SUNFLOWERING

BY BOB STANISH

THINKING, FEELING AND DOING ACTIVITIES FOR CREATIVE

IMAGINATIVE EXPRESSION

ILLUSTRATED BY NANCEE VOLPE

DEDICATION

**This book is dedicated to a couple of sunflowers that Pat and I cultivated —
Jon and Lindley.**

Published by:
GOOD APPLE, INC.
Box 299
Carthage, IL 62321

ISBN No. 0-916456-12-9

Printing No. 15

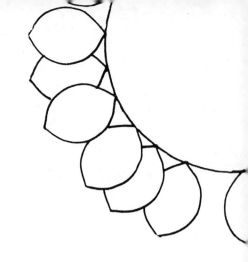

DO SUNFLOWERS EVER GROW TIRED OF REACHING TO THE SUN?

DO SUNFLOWERS EVER WISH THEY COULD SEE THE SUNSET?

DO SUNFLOWERS LIKE TO HAVE THEIR ROOTS TICKLED BY
    EARTHWORMS?

DO SUNFLOWERS FEEL AWKWARD BECAUSE THEY ARE SO TALL?

DO SUNFLOWERS EVER GET TIRED OF WATCHING THE SUNRISE?

DO SUNFLOWERS FEEL SAD ON A RAINY DAY?

Earl Stone

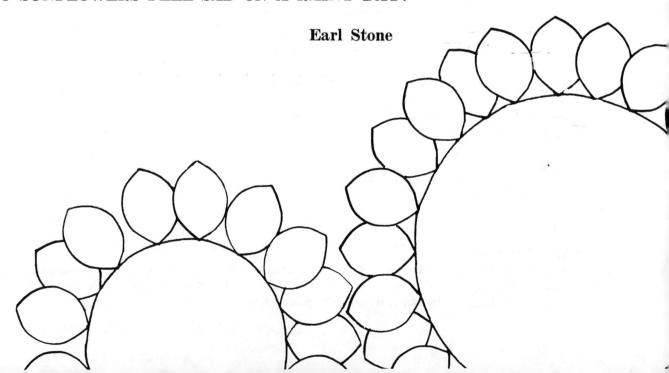

PREFACE

"Sunflowering," the title, softly identifies a process which I feel describes what Bob is about.

"Sunflowering" is the process in which a prolific, irreverent plant can grow and bloom under diverse conditions. This book is for those who care for children and the conditions under which they grow.

Through activities which encourage imaginary and real happenings to occur in the mind, this book deals with four basic conditions: (1) A relationship of things to things, (2) A relationship of self to things, (3) A relationship of self to self, and (4) A relationship of self to others.

Presented herein is a variety of activities which look at the similarities in the universe and in life in imaginative and explorative ways. Thus, per chance, to enhance conditions and live a bit more.

Troy Cole

TABLE OF CONTENTS

INTRODUCTION

"Sunflowering" allows for information to be played in the mind and altered and expressed in individual ways. Because of this, the book is for kids and adults. The adult thing with "Sunflowering" is the teaching ideas which contain a notion that knowledge, if it's going to be effectively learned and applied, has to be integrated into who we are, and into how we view and live life.

One purpose of this book is to provide experiences in thinking within the higher realms. Information does change with the advent of newer technology and investigation. Survival, within the next century, will be contingent upon applying the processes of thinking, not retaining large mind vaults of knowledge. To do so, would be to short circuit the mind.

"Sunflowering" looks at imagination and creative expression as the absorbing and applying processes for knowledge. A third strand, inherent in the book, is sensitivity. How well we absorb and how well we apply knowledge is dependent on how sensitive we are to ourselves, others, and to whatever we encounter.

Imagination, creative expression, and sensitivity are developed through the use of analogy strategies. The basic analogy used is the metaphor. The reason for this is that "Sunflowering" looks at everything as being interrelated. The chemistry within us is the same chemistry found throughout the universe. So, the book sings of man's kinship to the Cosmos. And why not? Within us is the dust from stars. Since life is viewed as a metaphor, all student responses to activities are correct. What is needed is to draw out the degree of association in unique and interesting ways.

The preceding ideas are encompassed by four categories of teaching/learning strategies, and they are

Imagery Analogy Strategies. "Think of another sound like the sound of wood burning warm in a fireplace, or make a list of things that sparkle under an evening sky." These are examples of imagery analogy. This type of strategy calls for an integration of feeling with past observing experiences, a way to describe the external world in highly personal terms. Similarities established are in a general category of a sensory area or combined sensory areas.

Object-to-Object Analogy Strategies. Strategies of this type call for creative and imaginative thinking in broad metaphorical terms. Looking for and finding ways to compare seemingly unlike objects provide outlets for creative potential and application. Examples include "In what ways is an amplifier like a gentle wind? How is a constitutional amendment like a chemical reaction? In what ways is a ball-point pen like a subway?"

Person-to-Object Analogy Strategies. These are strategies that call for the personification of something, in order to gain a greater degree of understanding of whatever that something is. In many instances, newer or greater usage and appreciation of the object results. "How would I think, feel and act, if I were an infrequently-used eight-digit calculator?" or "How would I feel if I were a fallen sequoia tree?" are examples of this category.

Transforming Strategies. These strategies promote the use of imagination to alter an implied or observed condition or object. This alteration may include putting the condition or object to another use, enlarging it, making it smaller or modifying it to any extent. It may include the imagined placement or displacement of conditions or objects within a situation.

Interrelated thinking enables us to develop a kaleidoscopic view of everything. In other words, original patterns can emerge from existing pieces. By altering the placement of things, unique and different information can result. Perhaps another way of saying it is that "Sunflowering" provides for original combinations of the known, not new combinations of the unknown.

Students, who view school programs as not being oriented to their needs, are usually embarked upon imaginary journeys anyway, so why not utilize this human resource as a learning vehicle? Imagination is both a natural and national resource. Evidence of this is in the inventions and products we use and whatver aesthetic enjoyment we gain from expression of human creativity.

But evidence abounds and the personal experiences of many indicate that imaginative and creative behaviors have been and are still discouraged in a number of institutional settings and this includes schools. Creative alternatives to accepted norms are not always received in warm tones of interpersonal regard.

Teaching behaviors. Accept all student responses. Realizing that their responses will always be "right" answers, students will become more imaginative and creative in their efforts. To facilitate student interaction and participation, it is suggested that open-ended types of teacher questions like "In what other ways?... Can you elaborate a little more on?... How do you feel about?... What other things come to mind in regard to?... Can you give us some more examples on?...," are highly recommended.

Using a soft voice and frequent pauses will promote success as much as anything with the transforming strategies. Pauses are extremely important after key teacher statements or questions. Time is needed for students to visualize an imaginary object or thing, and to consider their feelings about this entity.

Utilizing feelings, metaphors, and imagination to discover and use information in creative ways, is not without concern. This concern is grading. To place grades on the products produced through "Sunflowering" would be a disservice not only to students, but to an atmosphere of freedom where an unusual idea, a shared feeling, or the wonders of imagination are expressed. Assessment as to student development should be viewed through their interactions in association with the behavioral processes cited on the Intermission page of this book.

Some organization is needed in a physical sort of way. Many of the activities call for space in which to move around. Desks and other obstacles will have to be arranged for flexibility of small and large group participation. "Sunflowering" is not conducive to "sit-behind-the-desk" type of teaching. A "stand-up-and-move-around" type it is. Also, "Sunflowering" is more of a state-of-mind than a collection of classroom activities. The kinds of learning and teaching behaviors called for are easily transferable to any curriculum. So, the potential transfer is the most important thing in the book.

It is not intended that usage of all activities is made with a single class of kids. This is also true of specific items within many of the activities. In many instances, a choice of one or two items, among a multiple listing of items on an activity page, is desirable.

Format. This leads us to the book format. The book is chapterless and there is a reason. Some teachers like to start at the beginning of a manual or a book, and go through a sequence of page numbers. The four categories of strategies are intermingled so that a distribution is made, if a page-by-page rendition of "Sunflowering" occurs. For teachers who like to skip around, check out the "Strategy Mapping Chart" for strategy distribution.

Near the middle of the book there's an intermission page with some behavioral processes listed. Looking at this page, after some experience with the book, should provide a better understanding as to what's occurring in the minds of students.

At the end of the book in the "Notes, Footnotes and Other Things" section, there's additional information as to strategies and activities. All basic activities are a one-page effort for convenience, so the spillover is at the end of the book. The spillover isn't required reading, but it's there, and correlated with footnote numbers.

Most of the activities have additional activities called "Variations." "Variations" may be either extensions of the basic activity or alternatives. In many cases a "Variation" activity might prove more appropriate than the activity itself.

Scattered throughout "Sunflowering" are activities called "Quick Liners." Each "quick liner" statement can be somewhat of a warmup activity to begin a school day or to close one; a fun way to promote discussion on a thought-provoking level. Don't go through an entire page of "quick liners" in a short period of time. A lot of thinking and discussing can be generated by just one item.

Coloring pages in the book can be used for other reasons than coloring. It might be interesting to ask students to draw or pantomime sunflowers based on the caption provided.

Also, distributed throughout "Sunflowering" are quotes on imagination from known practitioners of various trades. Should difficulty be encountered from unimaginative colleagues and administrators on what's going on, just quote a quote.

STRATEGY MAPPING CHART

Strategy categories here refer only to major activity items. In other words, "Variations" that appear frequently on strategy pages may encompass different categories. The purpose of this section is to provide a means for balancing strategy selection. All four categories used with some degree of equalization will promote a nice repertory of approaches for cultivating imaginative and creative thought on a feeling and doing level.

Imagery Analogy Strategies call for an integration of feeling with past experiences and communicated in highly personal terms. Similarities asked for are in sensory related areas.

Object-to-Object Analogy Strategies call for creative and imaginative thinking in broad metaphorical terms. Looking for and finding ways to compare seemingly unlike objects is the requirement.

Person-to-Object Analogy Strategies call for the personification of something in order to gain a greater degree of understanding of whatever that something is. In many instances, newer or greater usage and appreciation of the object results.

Transforming Strategies call for the use of imagination to alter an implied or observed condition or object. This alteration may include putting the condition or object to another use, enlarging it, making it smaller or modifying it to any extent. It may also include the imagined placement or displacement of conditions or objects or their component parts.

SENSORY SUBSTITUTION[1]

CATEGORY: Imagery Analogy

Opening and expanding one sense to accommodate others is a way to touch life in vibrating tones and variations. Encourage students to get beyond the realm of judicial recall and onto a feeling plateau of experiences recalled.

PROCEDURES:

1. In what ways can warmth be seen?

2. In what ways can harmony be felt?

3. In what ways can tenderness be heard?

4. In what ways can softness be seen?

5. In what ways can serenity be felt?

6. In what ways can silence be heard?

7. In what ways can something full flavored be seen?

8. In what ways can a pleasant aroma be felt?

9. In what ways can a feeling be heard?

VARIATIONS on "Sensory Substitution":

1. Try describing visually-related items without sight-related words; sounds without sound-related words; tastes without taste-related words, and aromas without words related to the sense of smell.

2. Divide your class into smaller groups and assign each group a different item for a five to ten-minute ([2]Brainstorming) session.

RECIPE MAKING₃

CATEGORY: Object-to-Object Analogy

What kinds of ingredients would go into a "friendship" cake? Regulate your temperature to a nice normal setting. Sift together truth; integrity and a helping hand. Add softspokenness and sensitivity and mix well; then add a touch of personality — a knowing smile will do, and continue mixing until very creamy. Softly, and with care, pour the mixture into an inner chamber. Select a baking temperature and test for doneness. When done, feed it to the world.

PROCEDURES:

Have students create recipes for the following:

1. "Happiness" souffle

2. "Popularity" fudge

3. "A value" sandwich

4. "Empathy" dressing

5. "A sensitivity" salad

6. "Laughter" dumplings

VARIATIONS on "Recipe Making"

1. Brainstorm recipe names and select those appearing most appetizing. Create a class recipe book.

2. Add measurement amounts to each of the ingredients. Discuss why one ingredient would call for more than another.

3. Write a recipe or two in poetic form.

COLORING₄

CATEGORY: Person-to-Object Analogy

The mind is a keyboard of chord patterns. Harmonizing chords in an improvisational way can bring about new knowledge.

PROCEDURES:

Try some colored cellophane blotches. Distribute pieces, large enough to see through, one color at a time, to all members of the class.

1. Have everybody look through yellow cellophane.

   Say: "Suppose you could make yourself small and enter something yellow."
   "What would it be?"   "What would you see?"

2. Have everybody look through red cellophane.

   Say: "Suppose you could make yourself small and enter something red."
   "What would it be?"   "What would you see?"

3. Have everybody place the yellow and red cellophane blotches together and look through both at the same time.

   Say: "Suppose you entered an orange."
   "Think about the inside of an orange."
   "Think about what it would be like
      inside of an orange."

After a five-minute period of silence, have students relate their experiences.

VARIATIONS on "Coloring"

Use different colors of cellophane and enter different things.

QUICK LINERS
FOR A MONDAY MORNING₅

Quick liners have been planted throughout "Sunflowering." A prescribed dosage of one or two at a given time is fine.

1. List as many functions as you can for a wink.

2. Sit for a few minutes and imagine that you are a moth. What would your life be like? What kinds of things can you do that a human can't? What are some things a moth can't do?

3. Touch a piece of fabric. In what way is fabric like life?

4. What would be similar to looking down 45 stories from atop a tall building?

5. What would look similar to looking up 45 stories at a tall building?

6. If you could place only one thing in a house of glass walls to promote privacy, what would it be?

7. In what way could you use the letters in your name to make a design of who you are?

8. Imagine that overnight all the grass in the world turned red. What effect would this have on the unemployment rate?

9. What would happen if the letter "p" were eliminated from the alphabet? Pick up a book and see.

10. In what way would life be different today without daydreams?

WALK THROUGH[6]

CATEGORY: Transforming

Rain, snow, wind, heat and cold against our skin are common experiences. In a sense, each of these substances has a textured feeling all its own. This activity also deals with texture, but of a different kind.

PROCEDURES:

Tell your students you will have them walk through some imaginary substances. Go through the entire list calling out each new substance every thirty seconds or so.

Substances to take an imaginary walk through from head to toe:

1. creamy pudding
2. sand
3. used chewing gum
4. salt water

5. giant frosted doughnuts
6. jello
7. angel food cake
8. a field of giant cacti

VARIATIONS on "Walk Through"

1. Have students create a list of "walk through" substances and do them.

2. Have students create a list of 10 things they'd love to walk through or 10 things they'd hate to walk through.

3. Try mixing used chewing gum with sand for an imaginary walk through. Try mixing some other substances together.

4. Select one or two of the walk throughs after completion and have students respond to the experience with "I felt" statements.

JUNKING₇

CATEGORY: Transforming

This is an exercise in group construction with no predetermined goals. Begin the activity with statements like the following:

PROCEDURES:

1. Let's visualize a junkyard. What kinds of things are there?"

2. Have a student or yourself record responses on a blackboard or on an overhead projector.

3. "In what ways could we put some of these things together to form something new and different?" Have students be as specific as possible at this point. In other words, if someone wants to place a refrigerator door to bedsprings, have them describe how the two items would be joined. Continue the joining together of items until ten or more have been achieved.

4. "Who can give us a description of what our product looks like now? What name would you suggest for this product?"

5. "What kinds of functions would our product have at school? How about in our homes? How about a supermarket? Can you think of other places that would cause our product to have different functions? Where would you like to take the product — to what locations? What could we do with it if it had no functions?

VARIATIONS on "Junking"

1. Have students bring to class pictures on advertisements whose products might end up in a junkyard. Do the above activity by pasting together those objects into a new creation. Use the products created for creative writing topics.

2. As a field trip, take students to a junk yard and collect small discarded items. Put these items together with a strong adhesive. Paint it with different colors, name it and find an interesting location — one that would cause comments and questions.

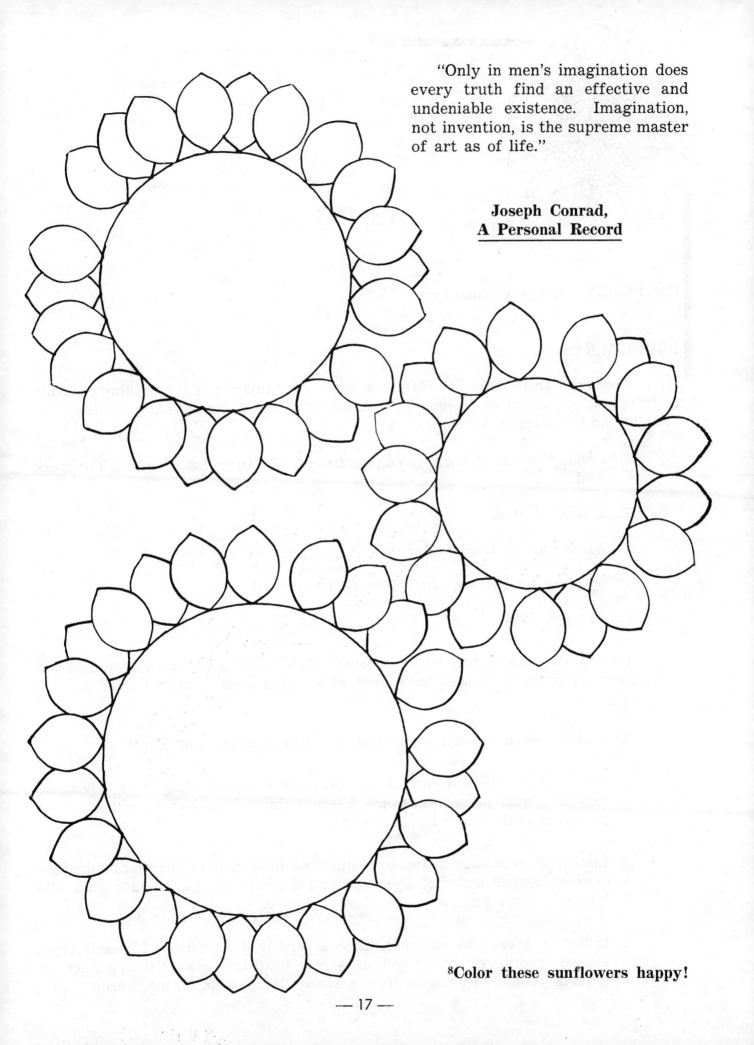

"Only in men's imagination does every truth find an effective and undeniable existence. Imagination, not invention, is the supreme master of art as of life."

**Joseph Conrad,
A Personal Record**

[8]Color these sunflowers happy!

TAPING[9]

CATEGORY: Imagery Analogy

PROCEDURES:

Imagery can be heard in different ways. Try this activity by asking students to bring tape-recorded environmental sounds to class. A five-minute rendition (or less) of the following would do:

.... evening or early morning sounds from a lake shoreline, river bank or creek bed

.... a wooded area

.... wind, rain or thunder

.... morning or evening sounds from a backyard

.... an open field

Inform students it may be advisable to place their recorders in a location and move away a hundred feet or so for sounds other than wind, rain and thunder.

As a class, listen to the tape-recordings without identifying locations.

1. On paper list ideas of possible locations for each recording. Check possible locations with actual locations. Discuss similarities and dissimilarities of perceived with actual location sites.

2. Listen to recordings again, but this time have half of the class tune into close-up sounds and the other half to far-away sounds. Discuss what was heard by both groups.

3. Using another tape recorder, tape a combined sequence of sounds from chosen recordings. Put together a new recording of continuity, such as from morning to evening or from a sunny day to a gathering storm.

ASSOCIATING LIKE/UNLIKES[10]

CATEGORY: Object-to-Object Analogy

Learning comes about through association of new knowledge with old knowledge or experience. Under these conditions, application can be made. Knowledge that can be looked at as having interdisciplinary application, is likely to stay with us, likely to be called upon frequently, and likely to be a foundation for whatever competency bases we develop and use. So, finding the "bonding-keys" of application from one area to a seemingly different area, is not only advisable, but creatively prudent.

PROCEDURES:

Take an example like gravitation. Rather than to ask students to recite a memorized version like "gravitation is the natural phenomenon of attraction between massive bodies," ask: "How might gravitation be like eating hamburgers?" A reason such as, "gravitation is like eating hamburgers because they both attract bodies," is a good analogy. The second question, if asked, is the key: "How are the two attractions unlike?" Attraction is the bonding key. Distinguishing between the kinds of attractions represents an association of new knowledge with previously experienced knowledge.

1. Try some easy examples like "How is a contour map like kite flying?" Possible answer: "They both deal with elevation." Elevation is the bonding key, so now ask "How are the two elevations unlike?" Another example is "how is an eclipse of the sun like a chocolate-covered peanut?" Possible answer: "They are both covered by something." Covered is the bonding key, so now ask "How are the two coverings unlike?"

2. Make up some more "likes/unlikes from whatever content area you're teaching. For interdisciplinary fare, try crossing disciplinary areas like "how is hydrogen like a silent "e" — or "how is a constitutional amendment like a chemical reaction?"

3. Have students make up lists of "likes/ unlikes" on their own as a chapter review.

IF YOU WERE[11]

CATEGORY: Person-to-Object Analogy

There are things we take for granted. In fact, there are things that have been with us for so long we don't even notice them. Take an eraser on a pencil. We don't pay much attention to it until it's worn down to the metal holder. Then all they do is scratch and tear our paper.

PROCEDURES:

By getting inside of things and thinking as they do, if they could think, we can learn much more about a lot of things.

1. If you were an eraser on a pencil, how would your body feel when new? When working? When being chewed on? When there's not much left of you?

2. If you were an eraser on a pencil in whose hand would you place yourself?

3. If you were an eraser on a pencil, what might be some other things you could do besides erasing? Which of these things might benefit humans the most?

4. If you were an eraser on a pencil, and suddenly had to find a new home, what would you choose other than a pencil? In what ways would this new home be beneficial to those who write?

VARIATIONS on "If You Were"

1. Have students list things they use, but do not notice very often. Select some of those things and have students become them. Write a story about how it would feel to be an unnoticed object with an important function.

2. Have students, by choice, write on an important function they have, but do not notice.

SPELLGINATING[12]

CATEGORY: Transforming

To those who see imagination as idyllic play, and to those who have never encountered "The Velveteen Rabbit,"[13] this activity is dedicated. Those who like idyllic, imaginative play and "The Velveteen Rabbit" can use it, too!

PROCEDURES:

Take any word your class can't spell and write the first letter on the blackboard. Take the second letter of the word and balance it in a funny fashion on top of the first letter. Take the third letter and have students suggest how you should balance it above the second letter. Then do it. Do the same with the fourth letter on top of the third and the remaining letters until the word is complete.

Ask your students to take a good look at how each letter is balancing and to close their eyes and concentrate on how the arrangement of letters is balancing. Erase the letter-balancing arrangement and have students write the word on paper. After a couple of weeks and without warning, have your students spell the word again.

VARIATIONS on "Spellginating"

1. Write a word in a vertical fashion on the blackboard and have students imagine a "gooey" substance like chocolate syrup being spilled over the top letter. Have them visualize how the gooey substance would run from the top letter down to the bottom letter.

2. Have students drop imaginary letters of a difficult word, letter by letter, into an imaginary paper sack. Have them take the letters out, one by one, beginning with the last letter dropped.

"Every mind is different; and the more it is unfolded, the more pronounced is that difference."

Ralph Waldo Emerson,
Essay on Quotations and Originality

Color these sunflowers with morning mist!

LISTING₁₄

CATEGORY: Imagery Analogy

A truly imaginative child is in touch with life. Kaleidoscoping imagery with feelings and producing ideas, he is standing among the flowers. Imaginative minds, like delicate blossoms, require time and space and special care.

PROCEDURES:

Cultivating imaginative minds in a classroom can be fun. Try a listing activity before taking a lunch count or before closing a day. Listing activities are designed to open sensory-closed systems. So don't judge. Let minds wander and create. These activities can be done individually with paper and pencil, or as a group activity, or with variation in between.

1. Make a list of sounds you hear at a given moment.
2. Make a list of things made more beautiful by age.
3. Make a list of things that sparkle under an evening sky.
4. List things that are lighter than a watch spring.
5. List things that crumple in your hands.
6. Compile a list of things that harmonize.
7. Compile a list of things you like to touch.
8. Make a list of mysterious things.
9. Compile a list of "squashy" things.
10. List the sounds of a department store.
11. Compile a list of wet things.
12. Make a list of things that chill.
13. Compile a list of twilight colors.
14. Make a list of morning things.
15. Compile a list of beautiful things.
16. Make a list of sour things.
17. Make a list of happy things.
18. Make a list of things that hurt.
19. List the things you love.
20. List things found in two's.
21. List things that reflect.
22. List subtle things.

QUICK LINERS FOR A TUESDAY MORNING

1. What things are weighty but have no weight?

2. Suppose you had a can of acoustical spray, what would you spray?

3. If you could give taste to something tasteless, what would it be?

4. What could you place in a cigar box for someone to see in the year 3000?

5. Which letters in the alphabet would prefer functioning upside down?

6. What represents the longest minute? How about the shortest?

7. If you were suddenly hospitalized and could receive one person you had never met before, who would it be?

8. What things could function inside-out?

9. What might be some uncommon functions of a ventian blind?

10. What is the funniest non-living thing in the world? How about the saddest?

11. How many ways can you use the word "blanket" without inferring a large piece of cloth or wool?

12. In what ways could you arrange a way to wake up at six o'clock in the morning, without having someone wake you or using an alarm clock?

13. What combinations would you like to see uncombined?

PROPERTIES[15]

CATEGORY: Object-to-Object Analogy

PROCEDURES:

Taking words associated with properties and applying them to feelings can be interesting. Don't run through all of these at once; spread them out, one or two a day.

1. What is the texture of a smile?
2. What is the texture of a frown?
3. What is the color of hate?
4. What is the color of love?
5. What is the shape of kindness?
6. What is the shape of a hurt feeling?
7. What is the weight of a promise fulfilled?
8. What is the weight of a promise not kept?
9. What is the size of friendship?
10. What is the size of loneliness?
11. What is the sound of happiness?
12. What is the sound of sorrow?

VARIATIONS on "Properties"

1. Do a collage on the texture of a smile.

2. Try the word "color" with each of the emotions cited in "Properties."

3. Picture an imaginary hat shop. What would a hat of sorrow look like? A hat of happiness? A hat of loneliness? A hat of friendship? Add other emotion hats.

4. Take the combination of 1 and 2, and 3 and 4, on the list, and insert the w o r d "more" or "less." In other words "What has more texture, a smile or frown? What has more color, hate or love?"

HUMANATING[16]

CATEGORY: Person-to-Object Analogy

Many products that we humans use reflect humanistic traits. For example: Programmed learning materials talk to us or to our subconscious. These memory retrieval systems spew forth facts that we are expected to grasp as we might grasp a handshake.

PROCEDURES:

This activity deals with the human attributes of products not yet molded completely in our images. Inform students that it might help to think in terms of almost being the product. Also, it might be a good idea to discuss with your class some general physical, thinking and feeling attributes associated with people.

Speculate on what human attributes could be added to the products listed below for improvement. Speculate also on how the lives of the product users would change with the product changes.

1. a drinking fountain

2. a cookie jar

3. a door bell

4. a metal folding chair

5. a typewriter

6. an overdue library book notice

7. a report card

VARIATIONS on "Humanating"

1. List products that have human attributes. If you could find the perfect person to match the attribute, describe what the person would be like.

2. List human-attribute-products that are annoying.

EITHER/ORING[17]

CATEGORY: Imagery Analogy

Reaching out with sensory tentacles to touch life is the metaphor within us. Choices of the inner metaphor may be subtle and very likely unheard. But, if heard, an awareness of self and others comes about.

PROCEDURES:

Try this activity by having students select their choice of the either/or's independently. Follow with a period of sharing, then a period of questions like "How are you like a wildflower or a flowerbed?"

1. ..... either a wildflower or a flower bed

2. ..... either a face alone or a face in a crowd

3. ..... either hues of one color or a palette of colors

4. ..... either a passing thought or extended dream

5. ..... either a stream or a river

6. ..... either a morning sun or a passing storm

7. ..... either the fragrance of lilac or fresh mown hay

8. ..... either an orchestrated sound or a single voice

VARIATIONS on "Either/Oring"

1. Do open-ended statements keyed from the above items like: "I'm like a river when I ...."

2. Have students come up with as many metaphors as they like to describe themselves.

ATTRIBUTING[18]

CATEGORY: Object-to-Object Analogy

Looking for attributes in any given thing requires observation, perceptual insight and critical thinking. "Attributing" is a small group activity, so rearrange the furniture, if necessary, to accommodate interaction groupings of five to six students.

PROCEDURES:

Instruct all students to bring a small object to their group. The object can be something in a pocket, purse or a school desk. Within small groups, each student will present his/her object and describe its unique attributes. After all students within a group have made a presentation, the group decides how all objects could be combined to form a new object with new attributes.

Upon completion, have each small group present its new object with the new attributes to the total group.

VARIATIONS on "Attributing"

1. Look at several architectural designs and discuss their various attributes. Which design has the most attributes? Does having a greater number of attributes make something more functional?

2. Do biographical sketches of famous leaders on the basis of listing their attributes. What are the attributes for leadership?

3. Look at various poetic styles or inventions or governments or radio versus television programming on the basis of attribute listing.

MACHINING[19]

CATEGORY: Person-to-Object Analogy

Using and developing group imagination to create a product is an experience with piggybacking. Piggybacking is the add-on to a single idea.

PROCEDURES:

For piggybacking fun, divide a class into smaller groups of approximately six students. Tell each group to select a machine and pantomime the operation of that machine. Tell them to work out the mechanics of it as a group and not share the machine's name with any other group.

If groups are having difficulty in arriving at a consensus, subtly suggest a pinball machine or an automatic car wash or a pop-up toaster or an automatic bowling pin-setter.

Provide time for each group to pantomime its machine and have the other groups try to guess what the machine is.

For an imaginative take-off on "Machining," combine two groups into one group and have them figure out how the two machines can be combined into one. Have them pantomime the new combination and discuss the benefits of this new union.

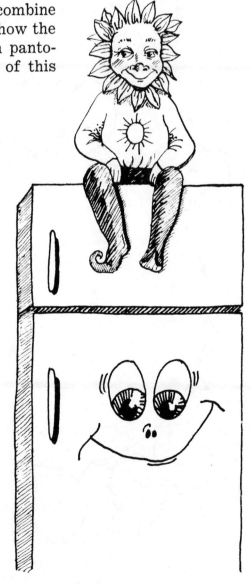

VARIATIONS on "Machining"

1. Have students independently put together ideas on paper as to what machines in the world could be combined for convenience.

2. Discuss not-invented-yet machines. In other words, what needs are present for which a machine has not been invented and what would these new machines do?

3. Have students select a machine or appliance and give it a personality in keeping with its function.

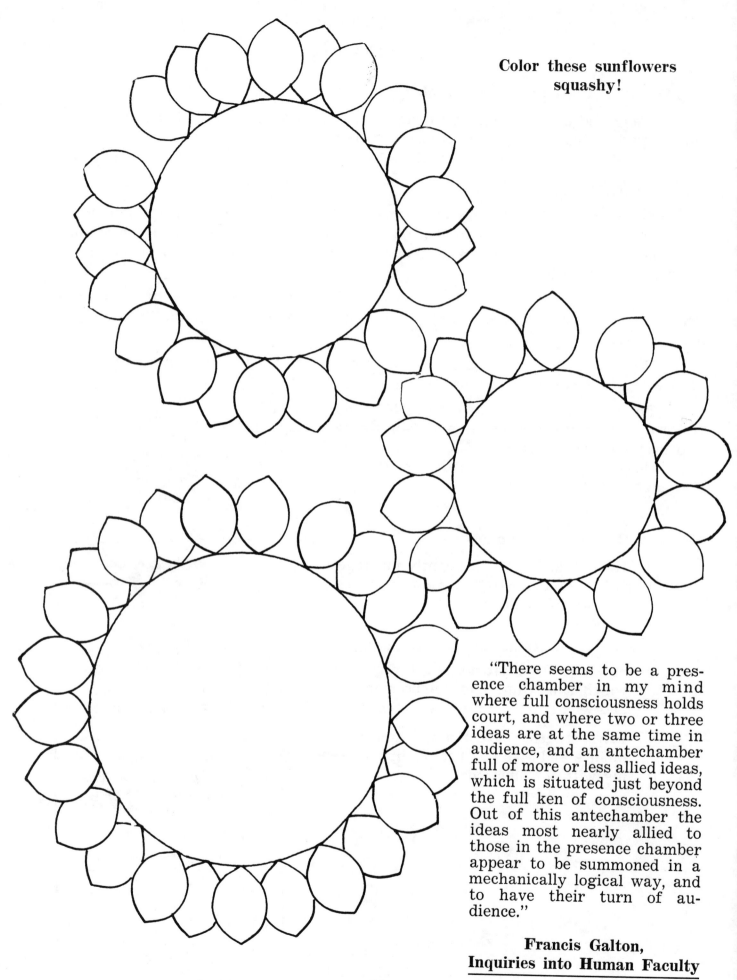

Color these sunflowers squashy!

"There seems to be a presence chamber in my mind where full consciousness holds court, and where two or three ideas are at the same time in audience, and an antechamber full of more or less allied ideas, which is situated just beyond the full ken of consciousness. Out of this antechamber the ideas most nearly allied to those in the presence chamber appear to be summoned in a mechanically logical way, and to have their turn of audience."

**Francis Galton,
Inquiries into Human Faculty**

FRAGMENTING[20]

CATEGORY: Transforming

Making fragments from different things into a new thing is an imaginative activity. There's a lot of flexibility here for unlimited imagining.

PROCEDURES:

Fragmented faces. Bring old magazine covers with human faces to school. Cut the covers into vertical or horizontal strips (choose one way or the other) and pile them in a heap. Have students piece together a new collage face. For real fun, encourage them to provide a personality description for each new face.

Fragmented machines. Bring old mail order catalogs to school. Have students cut machinery parts from many different pictured machines and put together a collage of a new never-before-invented machine. Have them describe the operation and purpose of the new machines.

Fragmented yummies. Bring old seed catalogs to school and have students create new vegetables or fruit. Have them describe the flavor.

Fragmented plants. With the same old seed catalogs, have students create new flowers and trees. Have them describe the new flower scents.

Fragmented animals. Obtain some animal pictures and come up with a new peaceable kingdom or a wild one.

VARIATIONS ON "Fragmenting"

1. Do all of the above and have students group a fragmented face with three or four of the other fragmented items for the purpose of creating a story.

2. Encourage students to discuss what things in the world they would like to see fragmented into something new and different.

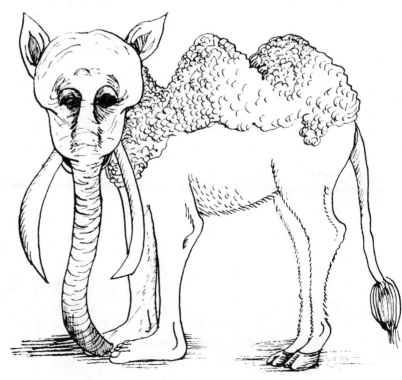

SOUNDS[21]

CATEGORY: Imagery Analogy

Our world beats impulses of imagery for those who listen. Listening, experiencing, recalling and comparing are the necessary skills here.

PROCEDURES:

1. Think of another sound like the sound of rustling leaves.

2. Think of another sound like the sound of distant thunder.

3. Think of another sound like the sound of wood burning warm in a fireplace.

4. Think of another sound like the sound of falling rain on a roof top.

5. Think of another sound like the sound of white water from a roaring river.

LISTENING

Have students, with eyes closed, listen for faraway sounds. Have them listen for close sounds. What faraway sounds would they like to move closer? What close sounds would they like to move faraway?

VARIATION on "Listening"

Take your class on a field trip and listen to the sounds of a pond.

SOUNDS FOR ALL SEASONS

What are the sounds of summer? -of fall? -of winter? -of spring? What changes would occur if the sounds of summer became the sounds of winter? How about spring with fall?

QUICK LINERS FOR A WEDNESDAY MORNING

1. List all of the things in your world that occur on a Wednesday. After listing Wednesday things, think of a Wednesday color. Think of a Wednesday song, and think of words that fit a Wednesday kind of mood.

2. What words would be more fun pronounced backwards?

3. If you were a human clock, at what time would you prefer your arms?

4. How could sunglasses be redesigned to avoid contact with a nose?

5. What question would you like someone to ask you that has never been asked before?

6. What kinds of ingredients would go into a happy life?

7. What words would you like to see reworded for the convenience of spelling?

8. If you could choose any animal in the world to talk to, what animal would you choose and what kinds of questions might you ask?

9. Whose shoes in the world would be the most difficult to fill?

10. What three common objects could you use to produce a shadow of a wheelbarrow without using a wheelbarrow? How about a sliding board or a t.v. antenna?

11. Suppose your job consisted of creating unusual ice cream flavors, what is the most unusual flavor you'd like to create?

RECYCLING WORDS[22]

CATEGORY: Object-to-Object Analogy

Words can be recycled in various ways. For instance, something that might lodge in our heads through thinking, feeling or doing may represent a symbol for transfer. The book, "Jonathan Livingston Seagull," by Richard Bach might symbolize something other than a book — maybe a way of becoming? A sentence, like "I hope to Jonathan Seagull it on a different level," carries an implied meaning in a picturesque sort of way.

PROCEDURES:

1. Give your students a few examples of the following and ask for implied meanings:

   "I'm going to downstaircase this feeling."

   "I need some help on sunflowering this thought."

   "I'll sandcastle it first."

2. Have students look for word-objects around them for recycling. Examples should be personified with personal pronouns, like "I'd like to bulletin board this idea."

3. Think about and discuss how many different implied meanings can come about from one word through a recycling process.

4. List twenty or thirty words of a technical nature, affiliated with a specific discipline like mathematics, or chemistry, or whatever, and use them as replacement words in a fairy tale or children's short stories. Be sure the words replaced in the story are taken out. This is a fun activity that can demonstrate effectively the concept of recycling.

MALFUNCTIONING[23]

CATEGORY: Person-to-Object Analogy

By becoming something other than ourselves at times, interesting techniques of problem-solving can be played imaginatively.

PROCEDURES:

As an example, have students imagine themselves as a stapler. Have them describe how they would look and how their bodies would feel. How their insides would feel when in use. How their bodies would feel when not in use. Tell them to imagine themselves as a malfunctioning stapler. If they were a malfunctioning stapler, what portions of their bodies might not be working? Have them list through brainstorming all of their possible malfunctions as a stapler, with possible causes. Be sure to have a recorder writing responses on the blackboard.

After a ten-minute brainstorming session, present to the class a malfunctioning stapler. This should prove no problem in most schools. Have students examine the broken stapler in relationship to responses on the blackboard. Through group consensus arrive at a possible cause. Select a few students to repair the damaged stapler, if possible. If not, determine the cause through observation and speculation.

VARIATIONS on "Malfunctioning"

1. Try this approach with a malfunctioning aquarium, or a pencil sharpener, or other unworkable classroom equipment.

2. Try this approach with other malfunctioning things of a different order — like a feeling of alienation, or becoming a citizens' council meeting room with noncouncil citizens in attendance.

BALLOONING[24]

CATEGORY: Transforming

"Ballooning" is a subtle way of teaching, sharing and disseminating knowledge.

Do a little research. Use an encyclopedia to find information on gondola balloons. A gondola on a balloon is a basket that carries people aloft.

PROCEDURES:

Tell students a little about gondola balloons and how some people used to, and still do, go up in them. Discuss the kinds of things that might be seen from a certain altitude aloft in a balloon.

As a class, imaginatively construct a giant gondola balloon, one that would accommodate the entire class. Decide the color pattern, its general appearance, and who the navigator might be. Have the navigator set the course so that a flight pattern would include a country or a state or a particular region studied.

Have everyone climb imaginatively aboard. Throw out the sand bags and light the burners. While aloft, have students point out certain landmarks, geographical formations, and describe the kinds of things going on below.

VARIATIONS on "Ballooning"

1. If studying contemporary societies and areas, try ballooning as a chapter review.

2. Try ballooning in teaching map-study skills. Placea relief map on the classroom floor. Have a small number of students stand over the map and describe the view below when aloft in a balloon. Point out river courses, where villages and cities are, irregular coastline shapes, agricultural areas, etc.

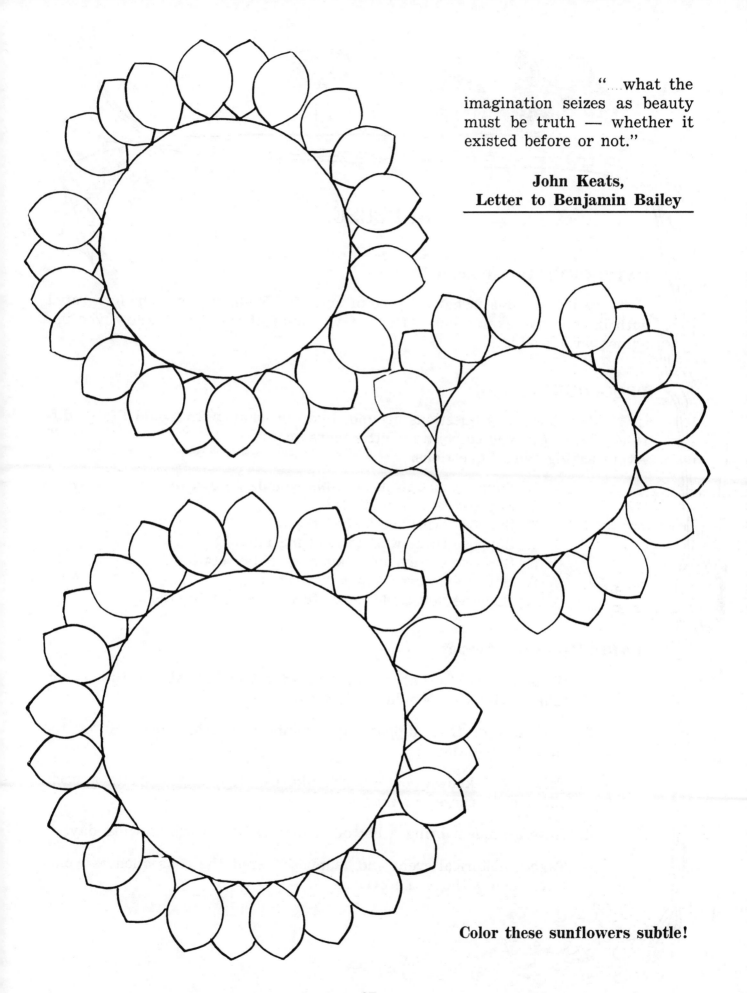

"...what the imagination seizes as beauty must be truth — whether it existed before or not."

**John Keats,
Letter to Benjamin Bailey**

Color these sunflowers subtle!

SUPPOSE₂₅

CATEGORY: Transforming

"Suppose" is a "what if" type of activity. Feelings should be integrated with imaginative expression. After a few rounds of this, you'll know who imagines with feeling.

PROCEDURES:

Sprinkle a few questions around, like "In what ways would life be different?" or "can you elaborate a little more on ....?" Avoid asking "why" questions.

1. Suppose mountain streams wouldn't flow.
2. Suppose leaves didn't fall.
3. Suppose everyone looked the same.
4. Suppose there was no morning mist.
5. Suppose the evening sky was void of stars.
6. Suppose no one knew how to smile.
7. Suppose you could never feel a summer breeze.

VARIATIONS on "Suppose"

1. Write a short story about the "leaf that wouldn't fall," or the "mountain stream that wouldn't flow."

2. Take one of the "suppose statements and brainstorm all of the changes resulting.

3. Take a well-known poetic style, like e.e. cummings. Write a poem about a "suppose" in that mode.

4. Have a student bring a list of "supposes" for the following day.

5. Take a historical event and "suppose" what the consequences would have been without the event.

IMAGERY PRODUCTIONS[26]

CATEGORY: Imagery Analogy

Integrating impulses of sound and sight can be an interesting sensory-affecting experience.

PROCEDURES:

Try showing a few minutes of a technicolor film without sound and out of focus. Distort the film so that images are unclear and colors blend. At the same time, play a classical or contemporary music recording. Make sure the film is land or sea oriented, and not people oriented.

1. Have students sit quietly and digest color with sound while thinking about the integrated impulses produced.

2. Share feelings and thoughts created by the sight-sound production.

VARIATIONS on "Imagery Productions"

1. Try showing two or more films at the same time with side-by-side projection screens and with musical accompaniment.

2. Read selected poetry with a particular sight-sound production.

3. Stage improvisational drama, such as mime with a sight-sound production.

4. Have students write short science-fiction stories and do a sight-sound production using the musical theme of 2001 Space Odyssey.

5. A stop-action-movie projector can create instant abstract expressionistic stills with an occasional stop-action pause. By sharpening the focus on these stops, the concept of impressionism could be taught.

6. Add an additional sensory-related area to a sight-sound production such as burning incense, or using a heavily scented room freshener.

WHICH IS?[27]

CATEGORY: Object-to-Object Analogy

These analogies have been adapted from Making It Strange,[28] Synetics Incorporated. Use your imagination in a way that amuses or excites you in answering these questions:

PROCEDURES:

1. Which is slower?
   (Red or yellow)
   Why? ....

2. Which is softer?
   (A rainbow or fresh snow)
   Why? ....

3. Which is quicker?
   (A memory or a dream)
   Why? ....

4. Which is funnier?
   (A triangle or a square)
   Why? ....

5. Which is louder?
   (A wink or a frown)
   Why? ....

6. Make up your own.
   Which is ....?
   (A .... or a ....)
   Why? ....

HOW WOULD I FEEL?[29]

CATEGORY: Person-to-Object Analogy

Weaving abstract notions and feelings into the commonplace, the unfamiliar can become familiar. Similarities are everywhere because life is essentially a metaphor. Associating likenesses, a metaphor can open the mind to fantastic excitement and illumination. The following activity is intended to affect a metaphorical state-of-mind among students and teachers.

PROCEDURES:

1. How would I feel if I were an amplifier for a guitar?
2. How would I feel if I were a rice bowl?
3. How would I feel if I were a gentle wind?
4. How would I feel if I were a whooping crane?
5. How would I feel if I were a heart beat?
6. How would I feel if I were an ash tray?
7. How would I feel if I were a hungry stomach?
8. How would I feel if I were a worn teddy bear?
9. How would I feel if I were a fallen sequoia tree?
10. How would I feel if I were a billboard?
11. How would I feel if I were a church pew?
12. How would I feel if I were a teacher's desk?

After selecting and responding to one of the items listed above, have students answer the question "What would I say if I could think and talk?"

VARIATIONS on "How Would I feel?"

1. Have students "move" or "act" the way they feel on some of the items selected.

2. Students who selected the same item could establish a verbal dialogue between the items.

3. Determine what the items have in common. For example: In what ways is an amplifier like a gentle wind?

INTERMISSION[30]

Now may be an appropriate time to consider what kinds of thinking and feeling processes "Sunflowering" has been cultivating. In a sense, the processes are creative processes.

Thinking and Feeling Processes[7]

Fluent Thinking consists of the generation of a quantity of ideas, plans, or products. The intent is to build a large store of information or material for selective use at a later time.

Flexible Thinking provides for shifts in categories of thought. It involves detours in thinking to include contrasting reasons, differing points of view, alternate plans, and the various aspects of a situation. A variety of kinds of ideas and differing approaches are considered.

Originality is the production of unusual or unanticipated responses. It is characterized by uniqueness and novelty. Responses may be considered original if they are clever, remote, individual, uncommon, inventive or creative in nature.

Elaborative Thinking is the ability to refine, embellish, or enrich an idea, plan, or product. It involves the addition of new and necessary details for clear and complete communication. It is an elegant response, an ornamented idea, or an adorned expansion upon things. Elaboration provides illuminating descriptive dimensions, leaving very little to the imagination.

Feeling processes would include:

Curiosity is evidenced by inquisitiveness, a strong desire to know something. It is exploratory behavior directed toward acquiring information. It involves the use of all the senses to investigate, test out, and to confirm guesses and hunches about the unfamiliar or unknown.

Willingness to Take a Calculated Risk is activity that involves speculation, prediction, wisdom and foresight. The probability of success and the chance of failure are estimated before action is taken. Risk taking is characterized by the will, disposition and desire to set greater goals in anticipation of greater gains. Consideration for the elements of chance, like the unknown, adventure, and a tolerance for insecurity are traits common to the risk taker. He may also be described as perceptive, inquisitive, intuitive and predictive.

Preference for Complexity is a willingness to accept a challenge. It represents a desire to work with or handle involved details, and an inclination to dig into knotty problems. Challenges may be in the form of intricate ideas, difficult problems, complex designs or complicated theories.

Intuition is a perceptive quality that involves quick and keen insight. It is a direct perception of truth or fact independent of reasoning processes. It is the immediate apprehension of the unknown.

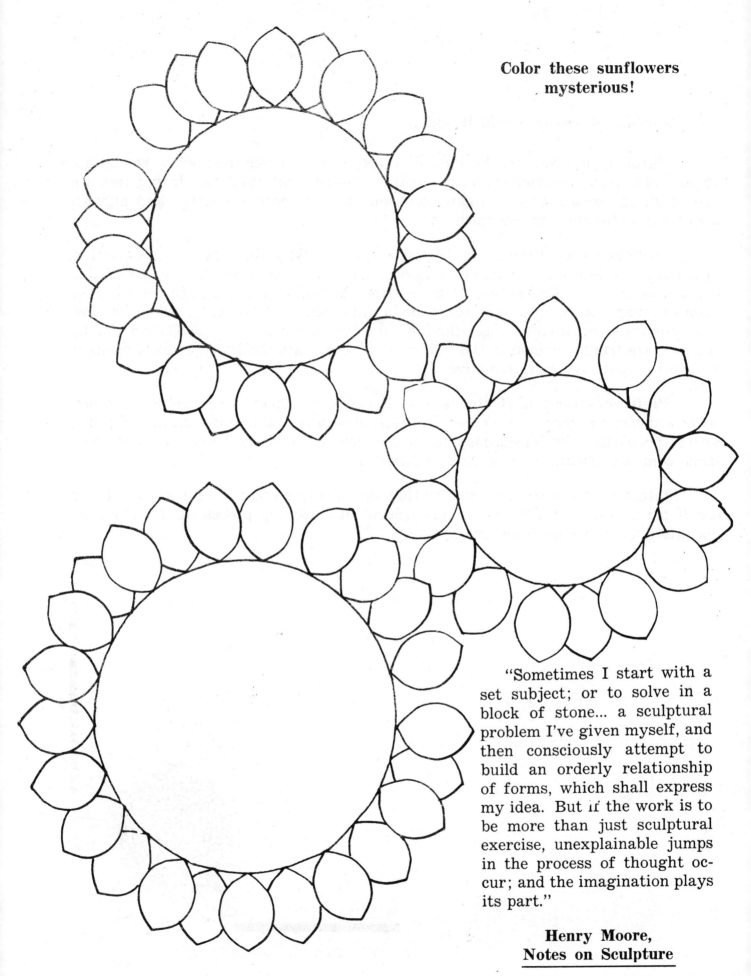

Color these sunflowers mysterious!

"Sometimes I start with a set subject; or to solve in a block of stone... a sculptural problem I've given myself, and then consciously attempt to build an orderly relationship of forms, which shall express my idea. But if the work is to be more than just sculptural exercise, unexplainable jumps in the process of thought occur; and the imagination plays its part."

**Henry Moore,
Notes on Sculpture**

SHADOWING[31]

CATEGORY: Transforming

Shadows produce interesting things. Have you ever seen sailing ships and dragons on your bedroom walls? By using your imagination you can create almost anything. Being able to make and improve comparisons is a skill that helps us create. This activity is somewhat like interpreting fluffy cloud formations.

PROCEDURES:

With an overhead projector, produce a light beam upon a classroom wall. Have students look for objects that might produce interesting shadows — shadows that would remind them of something else.

Take two or three objects that created unusual shadows and combine them to produce a scene. Have students speculate on what kind of a story would have a scene like that.

Encourage students to form groups of two's and three's and produce new and different scenes. Have each group create stories about their scenes.

VARIATIONS on "Shadowing"

1. Have students demonstrate how many categories of the same thing they can produce through shadows. Example: How many animal shadows can a single hand create, or how many geometric designs can be produced from objects found in a school desk?

2. Have one student read a favorite story, and have two students produce shadows of the story events as they unfold. There may be a need to provide some rehearsal time on this one.

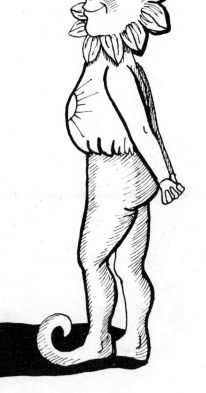

SENSORY PAINTING[32]

CATEGORY: Imagery Analogy

This activity provokes a carry-over from one sensory area to another. Try it as an assignment first, then discussion to follow.

PROCEDURES:

1. In what colors would you paint a happy feeling? What happy feeling would you paint?

2. In what colors would you paint an appetizing taste? What taste would you paint?

3. In what colors would you paint a pleasant aroma? What aroma would you paint?

4. In what colors would you paint softness? What softness would you paint?

5. In what colors would you paint the most beautiful sight you've ever seen? What sight would you paint?

The items below deal with experiences of a different type. Have the writer share them with you in an atmosphere of understanding and on paper only.

1. In what colors would paint hurt? What kind of a hurt would you paint?

2. In what colors would you paint an embarrassing moment? What kind of an embarrassment would you paint?

3. In what colors would you paint sadness? What kind of sadness would you paint?

4. In what colors would you paint a "I wish I were?" What kind of a "I wish I were" would you paint?

5. In what colors would you paint unhappiness? What kind of unhappiness would you paint?

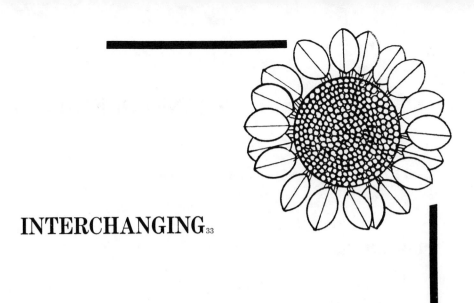

INTERCHANGING[33]

CATEGORY: Object-to-Object Analogy

Component parts can be found in a lot of things. Try an imaginary interchange of component parts among two different objects.

PROCEDURES:

Speculate on the changes resulting from each of the following interchanges:

1. Interchange a telephone dial with a radio tuning knob.

2. Interchange bicycle wheels with typewriter ribbon spools of the same size.

3. Interchange hydrogen with carbon in all of their compound forms.

4. Interchange the functions of the executive branch of government with functions of the judiciary.

5. Interchange the writing style of Dr. Seuss with the speaking style of a national newscaster.

VARIATIONS on "Interchanging"

1. Develop interchange strategies with whatever academic concepts you teach. For example: applying a foreign language rule to English sentence structure or interchange historical figures from two different eras or interchange cause with effect.

2. Discuss possible interchanges within a school system to promote learning.

TRANSMOGRIFYING[34]

CATEGORY: Person-to-Object Analogy

PROCEDURES:

Have students close their eyes while you read one of the two statements below with deliberation and frequent pauses. After a two- or three-minute pause of silence, have students write word impressions of their thoughts, then share feelings and ideas as a total group.

1. Imagine you are a sea shell glistening in the sun. Think of the hollow sound within you; of rain and wind; of a tide that rides you back to the sea only to return again to sand and sun.
   What do you hear, see and feel on beach sand? In the sea?

2. Imagine you are a feathery dandelion spore floating in the wind. Gently across the land you glide, guided in a direction you cannot control.
   What words would best describe the exhilaration of uncontrolled flight? Knowing that you can never repeat this flight again, what would you like to look for and like to feel?

VARIATIONS on "Transmogrifying"

1. Bring seashells to class and have students write character sketches of chosen shells.

2. Compile direct observations of dandelion spores. Use these observations in writing a descriptive paragraph of a dandelion-spore flight.

3. Have students contribute ideas as to what they would like to be for a few seconds in time.

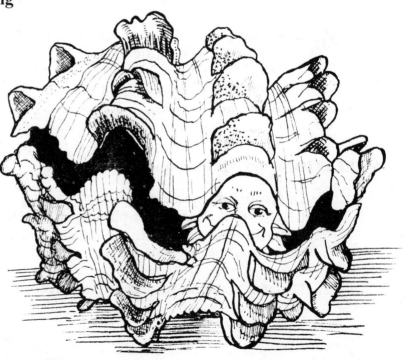

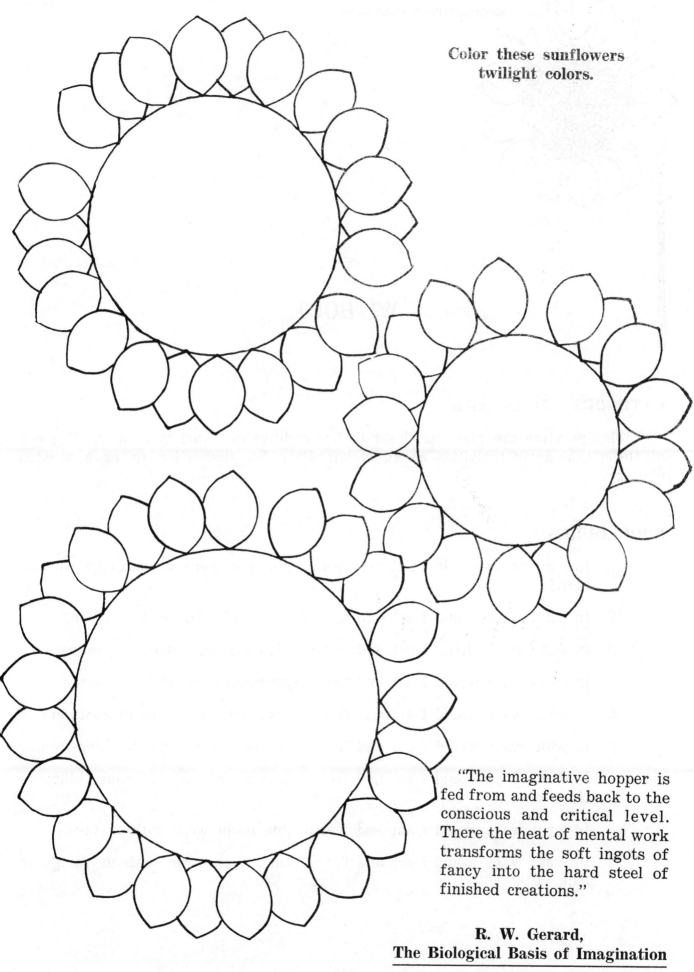

Color these sunflowers
twilight colors.

"The imaginative hopper is
fed from and feeds back to the
conscious and critical level.
There the heat of mental work
transforms the soft ingots of
fancy into the hard steel of
finished creations."

**R. W. Gerard,
The Biological Basis of Imagination**

WITHOUT 35

CATEGORY: Transforming

Imagination can place us closer to our feelings in a variety of ways. Try one of these take-away activities as an embarkation for discussion or as a written activity.

PROCEDURES:

1. In what ways would I act and feel if this room were without edges or corners?

2. In what ways would I act and feel if this room were without color?

3. In what ways would I act and feel if this room were without gravity?

4. In what ways would I act and feel if this room were without sound?

5. In what ways would I act and feel if this room were without sunlight?

6. In what ways would I act and feel if this room were without things to do?

7. In what ways would I act and feel if this room were without things to think about?

8. In what ways would I act and feel if this room were without me?

9. In what ways would I act and feel if this room were without things to look at?

QUICK LINERS FOR A THURSDAY MORNING

1. If you had to escort a visitor from outer space for a 30-minute tour of your community, where would your tour begin and end?

2. What kinds of adjustments would you have to make if everything you learned came from a book?

3. In what ways can hot be cold?

4. Which of your numbers would hurt the most if you were a dial telephone?

5. If all of a sudden you could stand only on your head and not on your feet, what things would look the same?

6. Which weighs more, a promise or a mistake?

7. If you could squeeze an additional hour into a 24-hour day, between what two hours would you squeeze the 25th?

8. Describe a bumble bee from a viewpoint of an ant. Describe an ant from a viewpoint of a bumble bee.

9. What things are seen more clearly from closed eyes?

10. Which is more intelligent, a period or a question mark?

11. In what ways could you remember a shopping list of 30 different items without writing a list?

12. If you could speak only twenty words for the rest of your life, what words would head your list?

13. If you were challenged to photograph something never before photographed, what would you consider photographing?

IMAGERING[36]

CATEGORY: Imagery Analogy

Imagery should linger like an illuminating sun. Gone for a moment and back again, chasing night shadows from an awakened day.

PROCEDURES:

This imagery activity is a pencil-and-paper one. Select one for this day.

1. What are the reflections of a rainy day?

2. What are the sounds of twilight?

3. What are the autumn smells of an afternoon?

4. What are the visions of morning light?

5. What are the night sounds in a city?

6. What are the tastes of springtime?

7. What are the voices of winter?

VARIATIONS on "Imagering"

1. Upon selection of a topic, brainstorm, as a group, words associated with the imagery question. From the list, have students write a descriptive statement or two.

2. Think of "ing" words associated with an imagery question.

3. Have students list experiences on paper cued from an imagery question. Turn the experiences into a short story or poetry.

4. Have students select a recording, or poem, or photograph, or painting that brings to mind an imagery question. As a class, listen or view it with discussion.

IN WHAT WAYS? [37]

CATEGORY: Object-to-Object Analogy

Encourage as many ideas on these items as there are ripples in a pond.

PROCEDURES:

1. In what ways is a ball-point pen like a subway?

2. In what ways is a rope knot like a super highway?

3. In what ways is a blade of grass like technological advancement?

4. In what ways is a leaf like inflatable plastic?

5. In what ways is snow like an hour glass?

6. In what ways is a soaring eagle like a light bulb?

7. In what ways is a mirror like a book?

8. In what ways is a river like a lithograph machine?

9. In what ways are wildflowers like an incandescent light?

10. In what ways is moonlight like jewelry?

VARIATIONS on "In What Ways?

1. Take the two key words in each sentence and have students list key attributes for each. Whenever there's a match-up of attributes, connect the two words with a line.

2. Take the two key words in each sentence and have students describe their functions. Show their relationships on basis of functions.

REFERENCE FRAMING [38]

CATEGORY: Person-to-Object Analogy

PROCEDURES:

When we see through the eyes of others, we see ourselves more clearly. In assuming the posture of something else, frames of reference vary dramatically. Try this activity in groups of three's, with each individual in the trio looking at the object through the eyes of the role assigned.

1. Look at tall grass
   .... through the eyes of an insect.
   .... through the eyes of a neighbor.
   .... through the eyes of on-rushing water.

2. Look at an old tree
   .... through the eyes of a poet.
   .... through the eyes of a nesting bird.
   .... through the eyes of a land developer.

3. Look at asphalt
   .... through the eyes of a root system.
   .... through the eyes of a parking lot attendant.
   .... through the eyes of an automobile tire.

4. Look at a can of dog food
   .... through the eyes of a starving person.
   .... through the eyes of a dog.
   .... through the eyes of a food chain store.

5. Look at a junk yard
   .... through the eyes of a real estate agent.
   .... through the eyes of an underdeveloped nation.
   .... through the eyes of a rat.

VARIATION on "Reference Framing" Determine how many different frames of reference can be associated with a given topic, especially a controversial one.

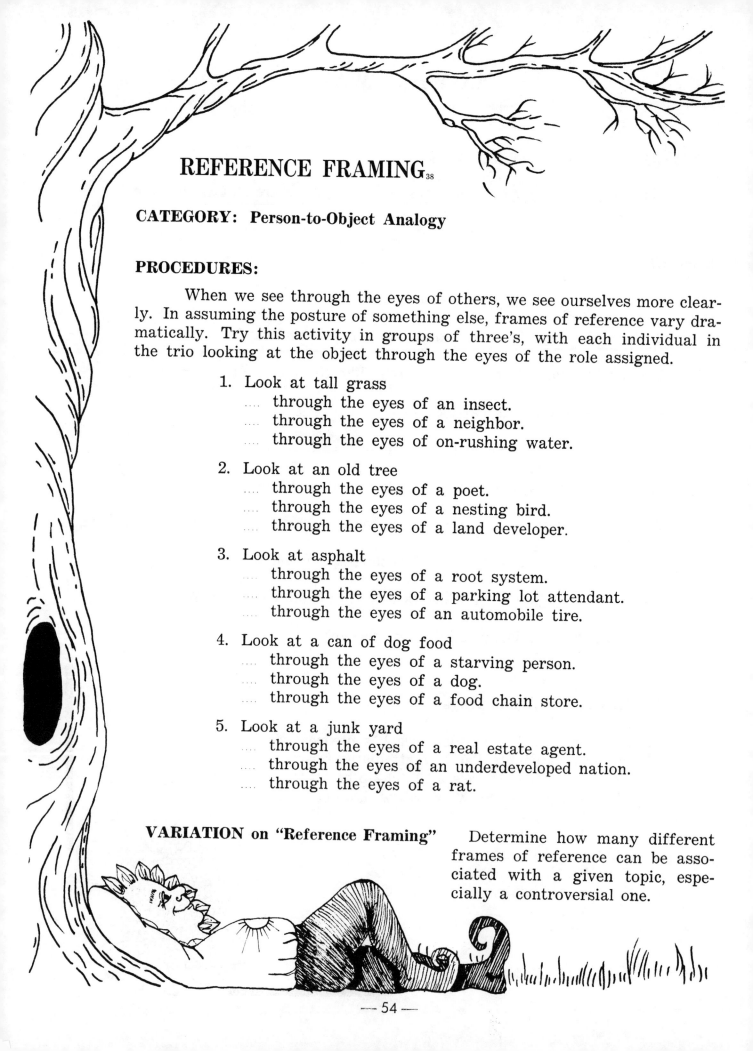

WHAT IS? ₃₉

CATEGORY: Imagery Analogy

What is tranquility? Tranquility is evening shadows, a silent snow, my head relaxing, a candle light, close friends, a summer breeze, a sleeping cat, a reflecting pond. What is loud? Loud is squeaky shoes in a library room, a tiger's stripes, a yowling dog, a playground, a hurt feeling, a summer storm, red and white polka dots, a mouthful of peanuts, a teachers' lounge.

PROCEDURES:

Divide your class into smaller groups and have them generate as many answers to a "what is" statement as possible, in a ten-minute period of time. Some suggested topics for consideration are

What is squeamish? Squeamish is ....
What is eerie? Eerie is ....
What is small? Small is ....
What is durable? Durable is ....
What is incredible? Incredible is ....
What is poetic? Poetic is ....
What is bitter? Bitter is ....
What is huge? Huge is ....
What is noble? Noble is ....
What is green? Green is ....

VARIATIONS on "What Is?"

1. Try brainstorming as a large group a "what is" statement. Afterwards, ask students to select the one best item in their opinion.

2. Try various colors with "what is" statements.

3. Assign statements individually and see what happens. For some insight try "what is learning?"

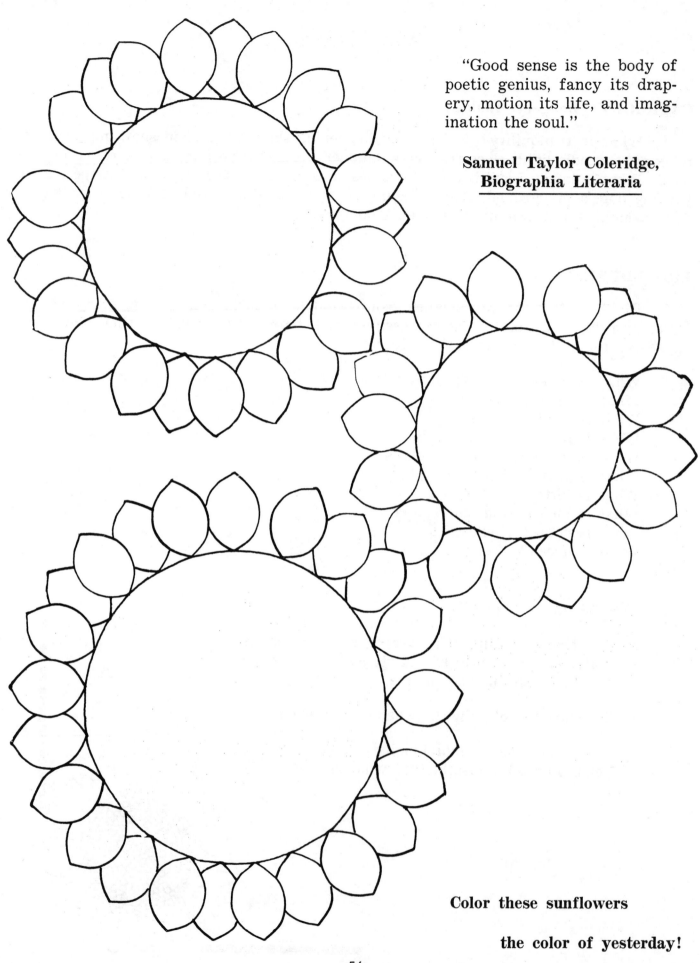

"Good sense is the body of poetic genius, fancy its drapery, motion its life, and imagination the soul."

Samuel Taylor Coleridge, Biographia Literaria

Color these sunflowers

the color of yesterday!

WORDING[40]

CATEGORY: Object-to-Object Analogy

Analogy forming is not always easy. This activity will promote concept forming in a fun kind of analogy way.

PROCEDURES:

Have students draw a series of lines running across a page of paper. You might have them draw six, but any number over four will do nicely. Now have them write any word they'd like on line one. Place a word on the next line that is related in some way to the word on the first line. Place a word on the third line that's related to the word on line two. Use the same procedure until all of the lines have words on them.

Students should share the first word and last word in this way, "In what way is (first word) related to (last word?)" Then use all of the words to show the relationship.

An example might be

barn   cow   milk   vitamins   health   happy

Possible explanation to "In what way is barn related to happy?" "In a barn is a cow whose milk has vitamins which makes me healthy. When I'm healthy I'm happy."

VARIATIONS on "Wording"

1. Draw a series of single word lines on a piece of paper in vertical and diagonal patterns. Make sure there's frequent dissecting of lines. Use the "Wording" strategy in the same way and have students cite analogies where lines cross.

2. Have students spin off on variation one, with creations of geometric design for analogy lines.

3. Try this approach with contemporary events, academic concepts, historical names or almost anything.

I'M LIKE[41]

CATEGORY: Person-to-Object Analogy

Metaphoring a feeling with an object is expressing the "who" of who we are in a vivid and understanding way. Use your judgment as to how to use this, small or large group or a two-way communication strategy between you and individual students.

PROCEDURES:

To give students a feel for it, try this example: "When I'm happy, I'm like my mother's best china. I shine and reflect and hear compliments about me." Then, this example: "When I'm sad I'm like a discarded Christmas tree by a trash dump, alone and down and without purpose, seen but unnoticed."

1. When I'm happy I'm like a ....
   Explanation:

2. When I'm sad I'm like a ....
   Explanation:

3. When I'm with people I'm like a ....
   Explanation:

4. When I'm alone I'm like a ....
   Explanation:

5. When I have something to do I'm like a ....
   Explanation:

6. When there's nothing to do I'm like a ....
   Explanation:

VARIATIONS on "I'm Like"

Try other opposites, like awake and sleepy, or succeed and fail, or state a conviction and remain silent.

GEOGRAPHINATING.₄₂

CATEGORY: Transforming

All of us from time to time have experienced the joy of discovery, of looking at something in a different way, of orchestrating a new image from existing pieces. Discoveries are like that. That is, they're usually there to begin with, but we looked at them in a different way and discovered something new. Altering existing things can bring about new insights.

PROCEDURES:

Take whatever country under study and roll down a wall map. Have students take a look at the country. In their minds, have them take an imaginary finger and follow the irregular shape of the border or the regular shape, whatever the case. As they do the imaginary finger tracing have them notice the features, rivers, mountains, cities, bays, lakes, etc., or whatever they might encounter. It's not important to remember all of the features, just a few.

Say "Suppose we had the power to mold or reshape a country like a piece of clay."

1. "What would the shape of this country be like if you pressed in the east and west sides of it with the palms of your hands, and in what ways would this affect the north and south sides? What would this country look like now?

2. "Now recall all of the features you encountered as you ran an imaginary finger along the borders. In what ways would these features be different as a result of this new shape?

3. "Would this new shape be more or less beneficial to this country?" "In what ways?"

VARIATIONS on "Geographinating"

Place a country in another hemisphere, or turn it upside down, or reroute the rivers and speculate on all of the changes resulting.

IN A DIFFERENT WAY[43]

CATEGORY: Imagery Analogy

Ask your students to describe the soft underbelly of a mushroom, or the sound of wind lashing against a willow tree, or the touch of an iris flower in bloom. We have a tendency to look, but not see; hear, but not listen; touch, but not feel. Among other things, this activity is about seeing, listening and feeling with the control knob on high.

PROCEDURES:

Duplicate the five questions below, and have students choose and concentrate on one for a week. Results should be logged in writing, and shared, as a group experience, one week hence.

1. What did you see today in a different way?

2. What feeling did you experience today in a different way?

3. What reoccurring thought did you think today in a different way?

4. What did you listen to today in a different way?

5. What did you touch today in a different way?

VARIATIONS on "In a Different Way"

1. Become an item such as an iris, or a willow tree, and relate what would be seen, felt and contemplated from spring to winter. If iris is chosen, think about the root as a self-nourishing food pack in the winter soil.

2. Be a mushroom in the same way, but include the cycle of creation and decay.

MY TURN/YOUR TURN[44]

CATEGORY: Object-to-Object Analogy

Looking for and finding similarities in life is a characteristic of the imaginative and creative person. Move the desks aside for this one. It's a stand-up and move-about activity.

PROCEDURES:

Introduce this activity by pantomiming the human use of an object. After a few seconds, transform the object to a different, but associated, object, then to a third, fourth, etc.

Example: Pantomime swinging a golf club. After several swings, switch the golf club to a rod and reel, and pantomime fly casting. Change the fly casting movements to throwing a lasso. After the demonstration, have students guess what objects you were pantomiming.

Place your class into small groups of six to eight students. Have one student in each group begin the activity by pantomiming the use of an object. After a few seconds, the student throws the object to another person in the group, who continues the same pantomime for a few seconds, and then changes it to another object. Continue changing the objects within each group until it becomes difficult to think of related objects. Remind students to think of similar characteristics when they do this activity. In other words, the golf swing, in the example, is somewhat similar to fly casting; the lariat can be similar to the movement of fly casting.

VARIATION on "My Turn/Your Turn"

Have one small group construct an imaginary project. This project is then transported to another group who will refine the project; then to a third group for further refining. Discuss the completed project and group reactions to the "refining process."

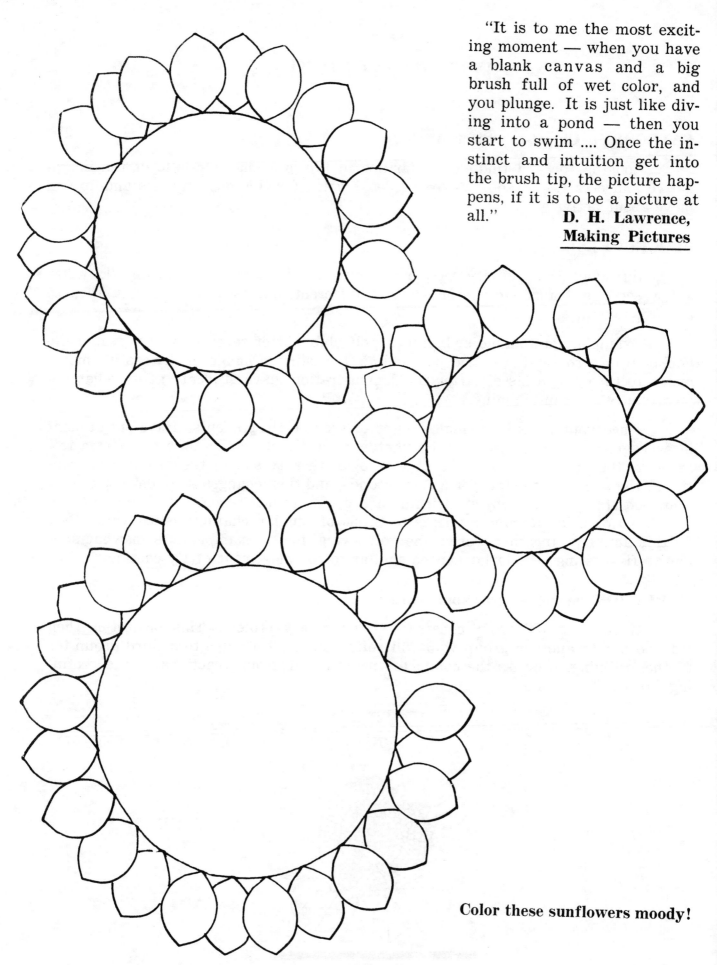

"It is to me the most exciting moment — when you have a blank canvas and a big brush full of wet color, and you plunge. It is just like diving into a pond — then you start to swim .... Once the instinct and intuition get into the brush tip, the picture happens, if it is to be a picture at all." **D. H. Lawrence, Making Pictures**

Color these sunflowers moody!

GROUP FANTASIA ₄₅

CATEGORY: Person-to-Object Analogy

PROCEDURES:

As a group fantasy experience, have students sit in a small group circle with their backs to the center. Begin the fantasy with a short statement, setting the scene. Students should add to your statement with their own statements of imagery. After a few minutes, stop the exercise and have one student summarize the group-created fantasy.

Some possible ideas to initiate this activity are

1. "I am a piece of driftwood floating on a slow river current."

2. "I am a flower bud about to open my petals to a morning sun."

3. "I am a hawk in glided flight between canyon walls."

4. "I am a sponge resting on a kitchen counter."

VARIATIONS on "Group Fantasia"

1. Try a group fantasia strategy with one of the activity statements in "Transmorgrifying."

2. Have students think of "ing" words to describe the experiences associated with one of the activity statements.

3. Have students create one sentence statements that begin with "I am like a piece of driftwood when I ....," or from one of the other provided statements.

4. Do a group interview with one student assuming the role of one of the four objects listed, i.e., a piece of driftwood, a flower bud, a hawk in flight, or a sponge.

QUICK LINERS FOR A FRIDAY MORNING

1. What if all of the triangles in the world were replaced with squares? How would our lives be different?

2. If you could limit the use of plastic to one product, what product would it be? If you could take plastic out of any product, what product would it be?

3. If you could make anything in the world larger, what would it be?

4. Think of numerals one through nine. Which numeral design could you improve, on the basis of writing convenience?

5. Think of the texture of sandpaper. What make-believe "ing" word could you invent to describe its texture?

6. Imagine nothing was black or white. What kinds of adjustments would we have to make?

7. Think of a chain of firecrackers exploding. What human event is like a chain of firecrackers exploding?

8. What is the personality of a morning glory? What is the personality of a walnut? In what ways are the personalities of a walnut and a morning glory compatible? Not compatible?

9. Other than in humans and animals, where else could you find teeth?

10. How many rectangles can you get from folding a single piece of paper?

MOVIES WITHOUT SIGHT.46

CATEGORY: Transforming

A few decades ago, a lot of imagination was possible by just turning the radio on. Radio drama was not only an art form, but an exercise in imaginative thinking.

PROCEDURES:

Try showing a film with sound only (no picture). Be sure and pick a film with some degree of dramatic dialogue. Have students jot on paper impressions of the major characters, scenery, and other characteristics listened to, but not seen.

Now show the film again with sound and picture. Students should check their impressions with what they see.

1. Ask students to share their imagined happenings with the visual account.

2. Ask "Suppose you were responsible for making this film. Would you cast the same actors, or actors resembling those you had imagined?"

3. Ask "Suppose you were responsible for making the scenery in this film. Would your scenes resemble more what you had imagined, or what you saw?"

VARIATIONS on "Movies Without Sight"

1. Many of the old radio dramas are now available on recordings in record shops. Get a hold of one like "The Shadow" and play it in class.

2. Do some research on how sound effects were produced on the old radio dramas. Share this information with your class and have them produce a radio drama script. Be sure and tape it.

GOING BACK [47]

CATEGORY: Transforming

Being able to imagine and contemplate the past can be as exciting as pondering the future. Set the stage for this one by having students clear their minds of present thoughts, by having them relax, and by having them listen to your voice with closed eyes.

The following script is provided:

"Imagine yourself in darkness, alone, cold, and listening to forest sounds. There are no cities, no civilizations. Just you without a language, without protection and alone. Think about your loneliness, your hunger, and the four-legged day creatures asleep in the night.

You sleep, but awake to the smell of fire. You see reflections of light between the silhouetted blackness of trees. With a walk burdened by drowsiness, you approach the light source. In a circle, and sitting, are likenesses of you. You are not seen, but you consider a possibility ...."

1. Have students finish the story in their minds. Tell them to think about their feelings and reactions as they imagine a conclusion.

2. After a five-minute interlude of silence, have students share their stories, feelings and thoughts.

VARIATIONS on "Going Back"

1. Write a preface script to the Wright Brothers venture at Kitty Hawk, N.C., or Lee's surrender at Appomattox, or any historical event. Place the "you" in the story as a spectator at the event itself.

2. Have students provide a "Going Back" script for something currently being studied, or as an element of content review.

PREAMBLING[48]

CATEGORY: Person-to-Object Analogy

Feelings are integrated with whatever we do. Yet, many individuals find it difficult to verbalize a feeling. Affective communication is essential to the imaginative and creative student. Accommodating and nourishing this talent is suggested through "Preambling." Sketching sand illusions for an in-coming tide, or watching wayward kites, and the sharing of those related feelings are preambling kinds of activities.

PROCEDURES:

Have students react to the statements below in terms of what they would probably see, feel and do.

1. You're in the vastness of space. Traveling with galaxies, you are free to search the boundaries of infinity.

2. You are a metal spring, coiling, and expanding, and bouncing to unbelievable heights.

3. You're a sand crab racing against an incoming tide.

4. You're a passenger pigeon in the Smithsonian Institution.

VARIATIONS on "Preambling"

1. Have students recall experiences in which similar feelings were felt in association with one of the above items.

2. Elicit student feelings through stanzas of music, lines of poetry or prose, or other graphic material. Have them relate other experiences that promoted similar feelings.

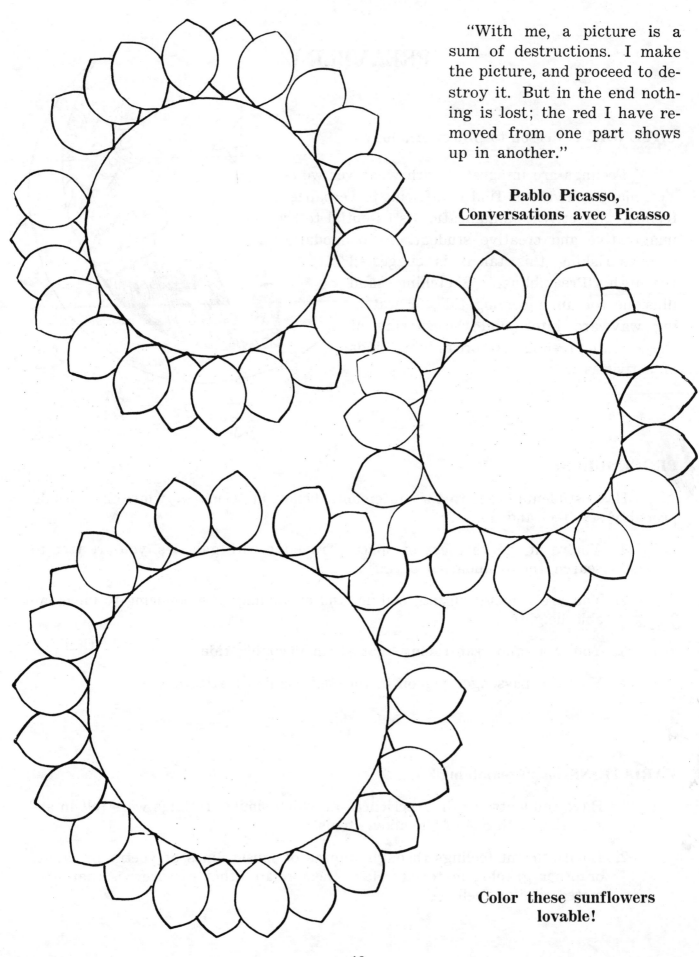

"With me, a picture is a sum of destructions. I make the picture, and proceed to destroy it. But in the end nothing is lost; the red I have removed from one part shows up in another."

**Pablo Picasso,
Conversations avec Picasso**

**Color these sunflowers
lovable!**

IMMERSING[49]

CATEGORY: Transforming

By attempting to enter a product, we can gain a better understanding of the product itself and the producer. This activity is conducive to certain kinds of paintings, and many other kinds of visual products.

PROCEDURES:

Select a copy of something like Van Gogh's "Potato Eaters," or George Seurat's "A Sunday Afternoon at The Grande Jatte," or any copy of a well-known painting with scenes of people.

Introductory questioning: "How long ago was this painting made? Take a look at some of the people in this painting. Select one. How do you think this person is feeling? What is this person hearing? Seeing? If these people were talking to each other, what would they be saying? What is the feeling of the group?"

Activity questioning: "Now sit quietly for a few minutes and close your eyes. Let yourself enter the picture. How do you feel being there? Which of the people there are you next to? Who in the group are you talking to? What is the feeling of this person? Now open your eyes."

1. "What would you like to say about this painting?"

2. "Does using the painting allow you to see more? In what ways?"

3. "What do you think the artist was thinking when he decided to paint this subject? Does it really matter to us what he was thinking about?"

VARIATION on "Immersing"

Take a contemporary news photograph or picture from a text book and do "Immersing."

IMMERSING OPUS 2₅₀

CATEGORY: Transforming

This activity also deals with the use of imagination to better understand and appreciate a painting. Try this one with a copy of a Picasso, Mondrian or a Klee or something extremely contemporary.

PROCEDURES:

Provide a full view of the painting to all members of your class. Tell your students to sit very quietly, and use their imaginations in ways you'll tell them.

Activity questioning:

"Look at this painting. Reach out with your imagination and gather it in. Let it grow within you. Enjoy the flow of lines, of shapes, of colors. Sense the warmth and coldness of the colors; know the strength and weakness of lines and shapes. Enter the painting with your mind; become a part of it. Close your eyes and see the total painting in your mind. See the lines, shapes and colors. See their relationships. If portions of the painting are not clear, open your eyes and look at the missing parts. Close your eyes again and see the whole picture."

Ask students to share their experiences of the painting.

VARIATIONS of "Immersing Opus 2"

1. Provide books of illustrated paintings and have students use the same procedures, independently, on pictures they select.

2. Take a field trip to an art museum and view paintings, sculpture and other art objects in the same fashion.

3. Discuss what other man-made objects could be viewed in this way? What non-man-made objects could be viewed in this way?

SPACING.51

CATEGORY: Transforming

This activity calls for imaginative construction. The materials needed are a soft voice, frequent pauses and minds that soar. Read each statement slowly so that thoughts will ripen and bloom. Before beginning, instruct students not to respond to questions verbally, only mentally.

PROCEDURES:

"Take a few seconds and think about space .... (long pause). Think about space as your space .... (short pause). Space has dimension. Dimension means size. How large or small is your space? .... (long pause) Space has form. Think of how forms differ .... (long pause) Some forms are rectangular. Some forms are round, while others have no definite shape. What form is your space? .... (long pause) Space has contents. There are things in space. But there is nothing in your space .... (short pause) Your space has dimensions and form, but no contents. You need to place things in your space .... (short pause) Think of some important things you can place in your space .... (very long pause) Now think of the things in your space .... (long pause) Add one more important thing to your space — you .... (short pause) Space has motion. Navigate your space. Think about where your space is going .... (long pause) What do you see? .... (long pause) What are you experiencing? .... (long pause) Now climb out of your space."

1. Have students share their experiences.

2. Have students recall and share what things they placed in their space.

3. Have students write a "Fantastic Voyage" based on their experiences with "Spacing."

UNIVERSING₅₂

CATEGORY: Object-to-Object Analogy

Within me is an inner universe forever changing. Like an outer universe whose galaxies light pathways to infinity, my universe is always brighter today than yesterday. Expanding brightness, because it absorbs what I see and feel and think. This absorption, additional to the physical properties of which I'm made, is my kinship to the Cosmos.

Within our galaxy is our solar system with a sun. All things on our planet can trace their lineage to the sun. All things are related, even the living with the nonliving. By reducing things to their energy equivalents, common analogies can be made.

PROCEDURES:

As an example, take a drinking glass and a shoe string. Think of a drinking glass and list all of the processes involved in making a drinking glass: glass - molten state - minerals - fossil deposits - the sun. Use the same process for a shoe string: plastic tips - synthesizing plastic - mineral (petroleum) - fossil deposit - the sun. What does a drinking glass and a shoe string have in common? It took minerals or fossil deposits or the sun to produce both.

1. Select any two seemingly unrelated objects and reduce both to their energy equivalents for analogy comparisons.

2. Have students relate which of the two items had the larger list of processing points.

VARIATIONS on "Universing"

1. Use the same process for a Person-to-Object Analogy Strategy. In other words, have students find the processing points of themselves and something else, like a star.

2. Try it with something the class detests, and themselves.

NOTES, FOOTNOTES AND OTHER THINGS

[1]**Sensory Substitution** is a rather soft and sensitive strategy. Interesting reactions will occur from students who fit this mold, especially when structured as a written activity. Student elaboration should be encouraged, but don't force response justification with "why" questions.

Setting the atmosphere is important. Try doing one yourself, in short phrase or statement form, as an introduction for your class.

[2]**Brainstorming** is a method for producing as many ideas as possible in a short period of time. **"Applied Imagination"** written by Alex Osborn and published by Charles Scribner's, New York, 1963, p. 156, cites suggestions for conducting a brainstorming session. These are well worth remembering:

1. Criticism is ruled out. Adverse judgment of ideas must be withheld until later.

2. "Freewheeling" is welcomed. The wilder the idea, the better; it is easier to tame down than to think up.

3. Quantity is wanted. The greater the number of ideas, the more the likelihood of useful ideas.

4. Combination and improvement are sought. In addition to contributing ideas of their own, participants should suggest how ideas of others can be turned into better ideas; or how two or more ideas can be joined into still another idea.

[3]**Recipe Making** is a fun activity. Additional theme variations are unlimited. Historical names and events written as a recipe, or book titles, or nonsense words, or special holidays, are all appropriate. Just stick a food title after the item you have in mind.

[4]**Coloring** is a beginning stage for other "Sunflowering" activities that deal with entering things. By imagining how something might look, operate, or feel from inside, we can gain a better understanding about whatever it is we are investigating.

Cellophane is an aid for this activity, but the purpose can be accomplished without it. Just have students visualize in their minds a particular color, then go through the activity statements.

[5]**Quick Liners** are intended as day openers, or day closers, or methods for breaking the occasional boredom of detailed desk work. Don't go through too many at one time, and never criticize an unusual student response. Encourage students to develop their own and, as a suggestion, bring in a shoe box. Label the box "Quick Liners," and have students toss in 3 x 5 index cards with "liners" of their own. Draw a few, at an appropriate moment for group fun and relaxation.

[6]**Walk Through** is the first among fourteen transforming strategies in "Sunflowering." The behaviors involved are generally the same as described by Alex Osborn in Applied Imagination, pp. 286-287.

Osborn's Idea-Spurring Questions are

Put to other uses? New ways to use as is? Other uses, if modified?

Adapt? What else is like this? What other idea does this suggest? Does past offer parallel? What could I copy? Whom could I emulate?

Modify? New twist? Change meaning, color, motion, sound, odor, form, shape? Other changes?

Magnify? What to add? More time? Greater frequency? Stronger? Higher? Longer? Thicker? Extra value? Plus ingredient? Duplicate? Multiply? Exaggerate?

Minify? What to subtract? Smaller? Condensed? Miniature? Lower? Shorter? Lighter? Omit? Streamline? Split up? Understate?

Substitute? Who else instead? What else instead? Other ingredient? Other material? Other process? Other power? Other place? Other approach? Other tone of voice?

Rearrange? Interchange components? Other pattern? Other layout? Other sequence? Transpose cause and effect? Change pace? Change schedule?

Reverse? Transpose positive and negative? How about opposites? Turn it backward? Turn it upside down? Reverse roles? Change shoes? Turn tables? Turn other cheek?

Combine? How about a blend, an alloy, an assortment, an ensemble? Combine units? Combine purposes? Combine appeals? Combine ideas.

Bob Eberle in Scamper; Games for Imagination Development, D.O.K. Publishers, Buffalo, New York, 1971, p. 14, rearranged Osborn's list to create an acronym: SCAMPER. Eberle's acronym is an easy reference and mnemonic device for classroom strategy development.

Eberle's Scamper techniques are:

S	Substitute.	To have a person or thing act or serve in the place of another.
C	Combine.	To bring together, to unite.
A	Adapt.	To adjust for the purpose of suiting a condition or purpose.
M	Modify.	To alter, to change the form or quality.
	Magnify.	To enlarge, to make greater in form or quality.
	Minify.	To make smaller, lighter, slower, less frequent.

P.....Put to Other Uses.   To be used for purposes other than originally intended.

E.....Eliminate.   To remove, omit, or get rid of a quality, part, or whole.

R.....Reverse.   To place opposite or contrary to, to turn it around.

Rearrange.   To change order or adjust, different plan, layout or scheme.

[7]**Junking** requires the ability to visualize unseen objects. A possible warm-up for this activity would be to have students describe objects in the room without looking at them, or have one student leave the room and have the others describe what he or she is wearing. In the activity itself ask specific descriptive questions about the junk items suggested, such as "how is the automobile fender shaped? What color is it? Does it have rust spots and if so, where? Are there dents? Where are the dents?"

The variations on Junking are especially appropriate for intermediate grade students. Individual collages of advertisement items are highly recommended for combining many objects together to form a different pattern or function.

[8]**Coloring pages** can be dealt with in many ways. Try reading a coloring instruction and have students draw, paint or color accordingly. Have them list other things that would fit the coloring instructions besides sunflowers. Ask if they would color the sunflower the same on a Sunday as a Monday. Encourage them to develop their own coloring books with each page containing a significant event in their lives as represented by a sunflower drawing.

[9]**Taping,** among other things, deals with noticing the take-for-granteds. Discuss the take-for-granteds in our world and how the world would change without them.

Recordings of nature sounds are available in many places. Try one with activity 2. Try a film that's nature oriented, by just listening to background sounds and not the narrator. The best approach, however, is to have students record their own, if the recorders are available.

[10]**Associating Likes/Unlikes** should be fairly early in introductory phases of "Sunflowering," as a procedure for formulating associations. This procedure may prove helpful for other analogy-type exercises included throughout the book. This is not to infer, however, that one single modus-operandi is the only alternative. There are many approaches for discovering analogies since multiple approaches to learning are in themselves numerous.

[11]**If You Were** is a take off on becoming a lot of things we don't normally think of becoming. Questions that follow "if you were" questions, call for insight and emotional transfer.

This activity will be somewhat incomplete if only the eraser-on-a-pencil item is used. It is highly recommended to follow the four items with "Variation" one. "Variation" two is, as suggested, a student choice item. As an optional assignment, by choice and handled verbally, make sure of the maturity level of your class. If in doubt, use it as an optional choice through independent writing.

[12]**Spellginating** will work less effectively if over-used. Use it with those words that cause students the most difficulty, or for a fun way to spell unusual multi-syllabic ones.

Another fun way of using this process for practicality is with a grocery shopping list of twenty items or more. Read off the list and have students place each item in an imaginative way into an imaginary sack. When complete, have them recall from memory each item on the grocery list. Challenge them to use the same process for real by picking up their mother's groceries without a list.

[13]**"The Velveteen Rabbit"** was written by Margery Williams and published by Doubleday and Company, Inc., Garden City, New York, 1968.

A few favorite excerpts from pages 16 and 17 include

"What is REAL?" asked the Rabbit one day.... "Does it mean having things that buzz inside you and a stick-out handle?"

"Real isn't how you are made," said the Skin Horse. "It's a thing that happens to you. When a child loves you for a long, long time, not just to play with, but really loves you, then you become Real."

"Does it hurt?" asked the Rabbit.

"Sometimes," said the Skin Horse, for he was always truthful. "When you are Real you don't mind being hurt."

"Does it happen all at once, like being wound up," he asked, "or bit by bit?"

"It doesn't happen all at once," said the Skin Horse. "You become. It takes a long time. That's why it doesn't often happen to people who break easily, or have sharp edges, or who have to be carefully kept. Generally, by the time you are Real, most of your hair has been loved off, and your eyes drop out and you get loose in the joints and very shabby. But these things don't matter at all, because once you are Real you can't be ugly, except to people who don't understand."

[14]**Listing** can be used in a variety of ways. Try it sometimes as a reading, without comment, or assign a Listing item to individual students, or to a small group, or discuss it with the total group. Try combining two items, like listing squashy things that hurt, or make a listing of morning things you like to touch. Combine four or five items and think of things that might apply.

Encourage students to create their own personal list of Listing; things they've encountered and know about.

Listing appeared as "Creative Listing" in the January, 1972 edition of Instructor Magazine. Written and submitted by the author.

[15]**Properties** can also promote the analogy of opposites. Try assigning or discussing the pairs of direct opposite inferences; i.e., smile with frown, hate with love, kindness with a hurt feeling, etc. Ask questions like "how are the textures of a smile and frown similar or dissimilar?" Then follow with "Variation" number four kinds of questioning, like "which has more texture, a smile or a frown?"

Try an addendum to "Variation" number three, by having students pantomime a hat-shop keeper, and customers engaged in trying on, buying, and selling hats of various styles and moods.

[16]**Humanating** can be highly successful if time is provided for discussing human attributes. Go into the attributes of thinking, as well as attributes of movement, and physical features including voice. Interesting reactions will occur with the report card item. Some of those suggestions you can take to the superintendent or the Board of Education.

[17]**Either/Oring** can be made more interesting if you try to predict how some students might respond to the activity before you actually begin. If there's a sharp contrast between your predictions and how they actually responded, take a few minutes and ponder the reasons. Students might want to predict how others responded, too, so consider this as an alternative as well.

"Variation" number one is a great one for predicting. If you go this route, be sure and have a group discussion on how some individuals were able to score high on their predictions.

[18]**Attributing** accommodates all of the thinking processes listed on the intermission page. Spend a little time with each group to see who's thinking with fluency, flexibility, originality or elaboration. Go around again, and see if you see evidence of the feelings of curiosity, calculated risk taking, preference for complexity or intuition demonstrated?

[19]**Machining,** among other things, calls for group consensus. Observe how leadership develops as each group determines what machines are to become, and how component parts are assigned.

Time will be a factor here, so place time constraints on group decision making and demonstration. Should time allow, have a discussion on the activity afterwards. The "Variation" activities may be more appropriate for follow up on another day or another week. "Variation" number three is an interesting take-home activity to do.

[20]**Fragmenting** has many possibilities. Try, if pictures of American Presidents are available in quantity, to have some students place them together into a collage and make the composite face of the ideal President. Use the same procedure with ideal inventor, the ideal actor or actress, the ideal mode of transportation. Decide what possibilities among the many available would be fun to try.

Fragmenting can also work without illustrated cutouts. Try it as a written activity, too. For instance, what three individuals of the past could you combine to make the ideal teacher, or the ideal student, or the ideal politician, or the ideal individual for the twenty-first century?

[21]**Sounds, Listening, and Sounds for All Seasons** are three separate activities that deal with listening to the sounds of the world we live in, and since that world is somewhat different to each of us, different vibrations from different individuals will be heard. Emphasize this concept as the activities are discussed.

Poetry is a source for Sounds for All Seasons. Have students investigate what poets say about the sounds of summer, fall, winter, and spring.

[22]**Recycling Words** can bring about some understanding as to why the language of one decade isn't the language of another.

[23]**Malfunctioning** represents the possible use of imagination to solve practical everyday kinds of problems. Discuss with students the application of this principle with common items and items that would not be applicable.

[24]**Ballooning** explores the potential of imagination as an instructional strategy. Map study skills have always been recognized as a difficult area to teach. Although Ballooning addresses itself to this area, it can be utilized in other areas where a different visual vantage point would prove advantageous. By looking at illustrated one-dimensional things like geometric designs, or buildings, or inventions, or the kinds of things pictured in textbooks, students could balloon themselves into positions of looking at it from the top or bottom, sides, or back.

[25]**Suppose** represents an instructional strategy that can be used in all phases of teaching. Asking suppose-kind of questions intermittently in anything that's taught, is a way of ascertaining student comprehenison and divergent practices in thinking. As examples, consider the following: "Suppose the industrial revolution began first in South America. Suppose Newton's Laws were not operable. Suppose no revolutions were successful after 1700. Suppose adjectives were absent from the Eng-

lish language." In order to respond to questions of this type, students demonstrate their comprehension or lack of comprehension of whatever is being studied. Also, and perhaps more important, are the opportunities given to students to respond divergently or at wide angles to a discrepant event or situation. These opportunities are opportunities for creative realization.

[26]**Imagery Productions** emphasize out-of-focus film, but other interesting effects can be created with an overhead projector, a clear glass or plastic container of water, an eye dropper and food coloring. Drop a drop of food coloring into the container while it's on ths overhead, and project swirling strands of color. Add color to color for interesting effects.

Oil pigment added to a tray of linseed oil is another way of doing it. Choose some recorded music to fit the occasion. Add other dimensions to the production if you like, such as strobe lights. By concentrating on produced visual and sound effects, students will relate interesting analogies and experiences.

[27]**Which Is?** is an adaptation from **Making It Strange**. Encourage students to bring lists of their own Which Is?es to class. In all of the "Sunflowering" strategies there is no single correct answer, just a lot of answers. With each Which Is answer, have students explain their choices.

[28]**Making It Strange** is a series of creative thinking and writing exercises prepared by Synectics, Incorporated and published by Harper & Row, New York, 1968.

Synectics, from the Greek, means the joining together of apparently irrelevant elements. The joining together constitutes a metaphor. Metaphors are personal tools by which students can absorb and apply knowledge. The "Sunflowering" strategy, Which Is? is an example of the Synectics operational mechanism of Direct Analogy (Simple Comparison). For an analysis of Synectics read Synectics by William J. J. Gordon, Harper & Row, New York, 1961.

[29]**How Would I Feel?** contains a collection of objects to be personified. Some of these objects take on social significance when responded to and discussed.

As a mood-setter, have students think in silence on the object they are to become. Consider the shape, color, size and overall characteristics of the object first. Second, think of the kinds of people that would see or act upon them. Third, think of the object's feelings, if the object had feelings.

As an additional variation have students compile a list of nonanimated nonhuman things who, if they had feelings, would have something controversial to say. What objects in the world would be least controversial?

[30]**Intermission** contains a group of thinking and feeling processes associated with creativity. They were derived from the following publication: "Identifying and Measuring Creative Potential," Volume I, A Creative Program for Individualizing and Humanizing the Classroom, Educational Technology Publications, Inc., Englewood Cliffs, New Jersey, 1971. The purpose of placing the processes in the middle of the book is to have some strategy coverage prior to finding them. By glancing over the eight processes and reflecting on student reaction to strategies previously covered, an understanding of the kinds of creative thinking and feeling called for is somewhat more easily digested.

[31]**Shadowing** may appear more appropriate for younger students, but don't hesitate using it with older students as well. Being able to draw analogies through the visualization of various combined elements is a good perceptual exercise. Additional techniques are readily available in any classroom. Have students make suggestions as to new shadow creations from available resources.

"Variation" number one is an exercise in ideational fluency, if a five-minute time limit is used.

[32]**Sensory Painting** is separated into two divisions. The first five items will provoke many color suggestions. Colors suggested are somewhat irrelevant, but the items verbally painted are not.

There are many teachers who could deal successfully with the last five items of this activity openly in a large group. If you're one of these, try it! Doing it this way requires sensitivity of the highest order.

[33]**Interchanging** deals with the imaginary effect of causing something to be replaced with an unlikely substitute. New functions, appearances, and ideas will surface in quantity. Student reactions should be written, either individually, if assigned as such, or by a group recorder if tried as a group activity. Upon completion, ask students to suggest interchanges that would affect their lives the most.

[34]**Transmogrifying** is dependent upon student relaxation, concentration, disassociation and motivation. Try it in the morning, and away from afternoon tiredness, if possible. Another crucial element is a teacher's voice that's soft with dramatic and deliberate pauses, even after the slightest punctuation.

There are many other subjects appropriate to a transmogrifying type of activity. Try writing a short paragraph on being a wayward kite, or a fallen leaf caught in a whirlpool. Transmogrifying, by the way, refers to changing into a different shape or form.

[35]**Without** looks at actions and feelings together in "what if" kinds of situations. Although it is impossible to predict what one would do in unpredictable situations, it's still fun thinking about the possibilities.

This strategy is intended to bring about an awareness that action and feeling are really one and not isolated entities.

[36]**Imagering** is an activity for reflection and sharing of the world inside us. Embedded with sensory approaches, Imagering is for a quiet day. If poetry is a portion of your instruction, try this strategy as an introduction.

[37]**In What Ways?** is a strategy for generating a lot of student ideas. Encourage students to respond, and not hold back, as ideas form in their head. Should students have difficulty in any of the eight items, stop and take on "Variation" number one. As students progress on the variation, return to the regular activity.

What kinds of student responses are to be expected on this strategy? Here are a few from a class of high school sophomores: "They're both tubular. You can use a pen on subway walls. A ball point pen has a clip, you can get clipped on a subway. Everybody can use both. They consist of common chemical elements. Both are capable of stopping. They are longer than they are wide. Both can go around corners. Coils are found on both. It takes money to afford both of them. They both create friction. You can use both in New York. They can transport ideas."

[38]**Reference Framing** deals with how things might look to others. By adding how others might approach a particular problem or view an event, additional insight added to our own frames of reference occurs.

Another way of doing this strategy is to draw three overlapping circles on the blackboard. Make sure each of the three are connected to all three. Have each of the circles represent a particular "Reference Framing" item. Where all three join, place common observations viewed by all three; where two circles join, place observations shared only by the two and within each portion of a circle not overlapping, place observations unique to the "Reference Framing" item only.

The "Variation" listed can be a provocative one. Try, in addition to controversial issues, a children's story where expressed conflict is evident or a legislative bill which carries strong emotional reactions.

[39]**What Is?** is an adaptation from the "Peanuts" version of "Happiness is ...." Try the strategy again later in the year with "Variation" number three with a different listing of statements.

Other kinds of What Is? statements appropriate to this strategy may include the following: heavy, light, radiant, peaceful, beautiful, fantastic, soft and relaxed.

Vary from "Variation number three," and try "what is teaching?"

[40]**Wording** is a strategy for helping form analogies. Use it as frequently as the need requires. Be sure and spin off on this process to include subject-matter facts and knowledge. Wording provides for flexibility, that is, shifts in categorical thinking, but with an associative strand.

[41]**I'm Like** will provide insight as to how students view themselves in certain situations. Concept of self will be communicated in various ways. Although it is suggested for group use, it works well on an individual basis. As an individual written activity, this strategy will provide a more in-depth look at levels of self-concept. Some of the reactions will be heavy!

An additional variation would be to attach a second statement to each "I'm like a ...." There will be enough explanation when the two statements are placed together, so don't bother about asking for a reason.

[42]**Geographinating** will excite students with a high level of creative intelligence. By altering whatever we see, new data emerges with the old to form interesting combinations. It is not necessary to have an understanding of the old. This will come about through the transforming process. Map kinds of things are extremely suitable for this strategy, but a number of other content variations can be used too! Try, with your students, the reshaping of historical events, scientific systems, mathematical processes, and speculate on the effects created by the change. What should emerge is a stronger understanding of whatever object, item, or situation was intentionally altered.

[43]**In A Different Way** is structured for a closer look. The five strategy statements will hopefully, catalyze a poetic personified awareness of life.

The "Variations" numbered one and two, are transforming strategies on becoming, with student responses reflecting insight of what it would be like to be.

[44]**My Turn/Your Turn** is a creative dramatics kind of activity calling for ideational fluency and elaborative thinking. It's a fun thing, so don't be surprised when group laughter vibrates throughout your room and down the hallway. Some students will react somewhat slowly to the changing of one object into another, but they'll catch on with practice.

Return to this strategy from time to time. The second and third time around should demonstrate increases in student ideation; objects will be transformed in shorter periods of time.

[45]**Group Fantasia** is described as a group fantasy experience. The group interview suggestion in "Variation" number three would be more dramatic if the person being interviewed is seated in front facing the class. Try a person-to-person interview with the interviewer seated in back of the room.

[46]**Movies Without Sight** is most appropriate for short films since a rerun is necessary. It is also suggested that films where the story is somewhat unfamiliar to students be selected.

Movies Without Sight emphasizes the use of imagination. Discuss imagination as a means of filling the void of visual imagery.

[47]**Going Back** is dependent upon setting the stage for listening and imagining. Try setting the atmosphere by turning off the lights and lowering the shades. Another suggestion is to stand in back of the room and read the script.

The most important part of this strategy is the individual conclusions imagined. Allow plenty of time for sharing and discussing.

The "Variations" are possibilities for dramatizing those historical and other subject-matter areas that are dull reading when assigned.

[48]**Preambling** can also be presented by allowing students a few minutes to consider one of the situations in items one through four, then write a short story dealing with what they would see, feel, and do as the main character.

"Variation" number one can be integrated nicely with the regular strategy by asking clarifying kinds of questions: "Can you share with us similar experiences, or in what ways would these feelings be similar to   ?"

[49]**Immersing** is a transforming strategy that's good for pictures of realism or photographs. By entering all illustration through imagination, we become more familiar with it and, perhaps, more appreciative, too! Textbooks are full of potential possibilities for this strategy.

[50]**Immersing Opus 2** is the same type of strategy as "Immersing," but more conducive to abstract designs and nonobjective patterns of color and texture. There are plenty of things in life where functions are not clearly seen, but aesthetically there's potential for appreciation. Revise the questioning somewhat and try it with a quilt pattern, or glazed earth pottery, or unusual rocks, or even a cloud formation.

[51]**Spacing** was designed for individual exploration. Atmosphere and voice tone are the important elements for strategy success. Make sure that no disturbing interferences occur for about twenty minutes. Then, set the stage by telling students to relax and clear their minds of present thoughts. Closing their eyes at this time might help as well.

The script should be read in a soft voice, and slowly. Stretch out the long pauses to a thirty to forty-second period. Short pauses are in a fifteen to twenty-second category.

Additional staging can be accomplished through background music played on a low-volume setting. Try something like the theme from 2001 Space Odyssey. For special effects, try a darkened room, strobe lights, a clear plastic container of linseed oil with swirling dabs of oil paint, placed on top of an overhead projector, with the image projected on a screen or wall.

Many themes are possible with a strategy of this type. Whatever script or theme you develop, make sure that most of the image setting is left with students to explore imaginatively.

[52]**Universing** was saved for last because it is closest to a "Sunflowering" state of mind. While planning the usage of this strategy, start with simple items and not objects reflecting a number of different components. For instance, a shoe would involve shoe laces, rubber, leather, nails, polish, etc. Try items like a shoe after students have had some experience with objects of one or two components.

"Imagination is more important than knowledge."

Albert Einstein